IVE SIMPLE MACHINES

McEwen, born in California, has lived in the UK since
He has written four previous novels: *Fisher's Hornpipe*
), *McX: A Romance of the Dour* (1991), *Arithmetic* (1998)
Who Sleeps with Katz (2003).

eviews of *Who Sleeps with Katz*:

ic in the way of books that spread like a rumor, of books that
d and, years after they appear, find others who've read them
inking no one else has even heard of them. *Who Sleeps With*
n look forward to a paperback reissue in 20 years from the New
eview of Books and an accompanying rapturous introduction.
ait?' – *salon.com*

passages of this book I read ten times, and then called peo-
read again, aloud. *Who Sleeps with Katz* cries out for a world
h a man might live his life with nobility and self-respect. Its
ints are against the powers that would degrade us: Seattle, tel-
, girls named Debbie. It is a celebration of that by which we
ated: martinis, the city, waiters. And it is a meditation on that
ould do both: tobacco.' – Max Watman, *New York Sun*

Francis Picabia, *Parade Amoureuse*, 1917

To the Champagne Girls

THE FIVE
SIMPLE
MACHINES

Todd McEwen

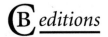

First published in 2013
by CB editions
146 Percy Road London W12 9QL
www.cbeditions.com

Printed in England by Blissetts, London W3 8DH

ISBN 978–0–9573266–3–7

MACHINE: any device or apparatus for the application or modification of force to a specific purpose.

The term 'simple machines' is applied to the six so-called mechanical powers—the lever, wedge, wheel and axle, pulley, screw and inclined plane.

The machine does not isolate man from the great problems of nature but plunges him more deeply into them.
– Saint-Exupéry

LEVER

This is a work of friction, and the resemblance of characters to any real persons, living or dead, is purely mechanical.

Mr Button Steps Out

CONDITIONS OF STIFFNESS AND STRENGTH

As in Archimedes' case, there was nowhere to stand—I was like those wooden statuettes you get in Africa, the little guys with the big diks. They're always rearing back, the dik jutting out, waving their arms as if they're thanking the moon for giving them such a braying donkey of a hard-on.

When I first got a real one, I mean one that was capable, I found myself hopping around in the bathroom, putting the dik into an empty cardboard tube from the toilet roll and thinking myself mad, a monster who would have to be tranquilized with a dart, captured by the police and destroyed for the good of society.

I figured the only way I was going to have sex with Francine, the girl I admired, was by chloroforming her in the bicycle shed. Of course she'd fall in love with me *afterward*—it was not honorable if love was not involved.

There were also Cecelia, Eleanor, Pauline. I imagined the dik was strong enough to lift all these girls, lift them up to the skies. I imagined it *lifting the whole school*, and it probably could have, the *steel rod of my absolute loneliness*, which while trying to fly proudly in my trousers also felt as though it was goring me, through and through. It created and proclaimed my EMPTINESS to the world; not my nubility.

ACTUAL ENERGY OF A SHIFTING BODY

Because of some kind of ancestral trouble, perhaps because my forebears either A) came from cold climates (Holland and Ireland) or B) committed awful crimes, the gods designed my dik in an impertinent way, which has caused me no end of trouble and grief. As if they had no ability to foresee, nor any sympathy for, the awful social exigencies of the gymnasium, the swimming pool, the army physical, they gave me a fully operational dik which, though, normally *retreats almost entirely inside my abdomen*. Perhaps they were trying out an idea on me: *let's see if it useful to make dik crawl up inside like balls when it cold*. Well, it's no use. But there they left me.

The mechanism they used to achieve this was a huge

spectrum of fears. These were stored in my parents and dripped into me, an intravenous feeding of fears, year by year, until by the time the dik got its benzine and started to function automatically, I was afraid it would be seen, that *I* would be seen. I was full of fear that I existed and would be noticed—particularly with a sudden and implacable hard-on.

In their wisdom, the gods gave the dik to me in a unique and maddening fashion. Imagine the pubic bone to be a kind of pylon, P, such as exists in the wing of an airplane and on which the structure of the engine is mounted. They took my retractable, cowering dik, which in truth is perhaps a bit longer than others and put it on a kind of fire-hose reel, R, so that in rolling up inside me the tip, T, remains just visible at the top of the pylon, P, prevented from disappearing inside me totally and perhaps forever only by an invisible and perhaps even imaginary restraining latch, L. The total effect of which system is to render me the uncomfortable, mentally unstable slave to a bulge in my trousers *when I do not have one for the correct reasons*; and to make me when viewed naked to appear to have only a *pink button* nestling in my fur, and no yardage by which I can be measured by the male or female eye. Though nicely proportioned and muscular, I have the *pipi Bernini* as far as most who have never touched me are concerned, and this may have driven me around the bend.

My trousers never fit and from an early age it was torture to buy them. I was so ashamed of the whole thing that I never *would* buy new trousers and consequently trying on new trousers became an eroticized experience and

I would get a boner which I had to wait on to go away; because of the pylon, P, trouble, they still didn't fit and the tailors, or I should say the man who owned the BOYS' SHOP, where embarrassingly I still bought my clothes, couldn't understand it. This was not a problem that could be solved with a measuring tape.

And of course the *old* trousers got too tight and the bulge even bigger. I was disgusting people, so I thought, with something that *both did and did not exist.* It is impossible to buy trousers, even today. I have to seek help and I'm too embarrassed to ask for it. I decided to grow a large belly which disguises the whole problem by crushing down the waist band and making *that* look like the source of my erratic trousering.

Discussion of dik issues with Cowznofski, one of my few friends in the early days of the dik: He approached me in some embarrassment in the schoolyard and told me that the day before he had caught the dik between the toilet seat and bowl in his home, in trying to sit down upon it. While expressing my condolences, I was in fact consumed with jealousy at this. If only my dik would *unroll* itself long enough to be caught in a toilet seat! I wondered if it was wrong to picture the exact length of Cowznofski's dik. He went around *assuming* this could happen to anybody?

So here was this fear we had of being priapic, at the exact moment in life when you ought, had, to be.

Francine sat directly in front of me in geometry, the highest level of mathematics I ever achieved—I think she was the same. I simply refused to study any more mathematics after that. I was worn out, though this was largely due to the physical stresses of being seated behind Francine. (They threatened me with dire stories of working in supermarkets, no college in the world would take me, I needed *trigonometry* at the very least to be a *human being* . . . but they lost. I went to Harvard and became rich *without high school math.*)

Francine was not the prettiest girl in school—in California there were plenty of blonde, beachy die-stamped beauties, all of whose eyes seemed to be the same color, and to operate in the same way, I guessed, as those of dolls. They'd shut their eyes slowly as you laid them down . . . of course what did I know about it, laying them down. But this was my guess. Francine was a girl you often saw in groups of girls, who *shuffled* everywhere, usually from the locker of one to the locker of another. You would see her shuffling home in the same group, in their flat little shuffling shoes, notebooks tight against their breasts, for reasons we could never discover. 'Why do they do that?' said Cowznofski. 'That drives me nuts.' I thought it had something to do either with television or with 'Betty and Veronica' comics. Sometimes you'd see the group of girls all sharing a cigarette with one hand, while the other held the notebook to the breast. Francine's mouth seemed perfect for smoking, I thought—she had mature-looking lips, often painted in slick orange or white, and slightly long, ever so slightly yellow teeth. She rarely smiled but more often sneered, especially where I was concerned. She smoked gently, letting the smoke curl up her face, where it caressed the contours of her nose, her flared nostrils, which I thought her best feature. She had somewhat ratty hair, but the feathered quality of her bangs and the uncertain lay of her hairline were fascinating, and sitting behind her I spent a good deal of time examining her nape, which was exciting. She had not a stoop, but a slight curve to her shoulders which I liked—possibly because it suggested some inner remorse, or submissive quality, although these were not traits she exhibited, especially as regarded myself. In winter she wore a short brown skirt, brown tights and brown boots—*de rigueur*—and in summer a tight, ribbed top, a floral skirt, and sandals—*de rigueur*.

It would be possible to draw many diagrams of my pain as regarded Francine and geometry, more diagrams than I ever drew in class. Plot a vector from the nape of Francine, F, to my eyeballs, E; drop a plumb line from my eyeballs, E, to my dik, D; measure the increasing inclination of the dik, D, to the underside, U, of my desk. We had these desks. They were from the 1950s and no one liked sitting in them. Each had a curved, paddle-shaped top of thick laminate—you were supposed to use the tail of the paddle as an arm rest. There was very little desk top space. There wasn't room for an open geometry text and an open binder at the same time. Everyone constantly dropped and knocked things over. You could say it was adolescent clumsiness, but it really was these desks. The geometry teacher, who was a real idiot, exploded with rage *every time* a pencil or a notebook fell to the floor, even after Cowznofski had kindly taken the time to prove to him that the desks were too small; he'd even come up with a *theorem* about it. Which got Cowznofski nowhere, except sent to the principal, for being 'snide'.

The desks had foot rails—Francine had a nice way of turning her ankles from side to side in her brown suede boots—but the point is that the desks were really too small for any of us; we suspected them of being left over from the primary school. Everyone had to *squeeze* in and out of them. And if you got the horn, staring at a nape, you were in fantastic trouble.

One day I sat behind Francine feeling doubly miserable, for not only had I been studying her hair and her curved shoulders and her corduroy indifference, the dik *straining* against the bite of the zipper and the unforgiving laminate of the squinchy desk, but it was February and I had a streaming cold, the kind which produces so much mucus in your nose and so much phlegm in your throat and so much rheum in your eyes that you cannot attend to it in class, for the noise you will cause and the always unwanted attention you will attract. You just have to sit there, filling up like a caldera of shit, for *fifty minutes.*

For some reason the teacher was getting through to me—we were studying trajectory, which is part of physics. Isn't it? We were to *make up our own problem*, a phrase which always filled me with a feeling of profound irony.

Suddenly I knew this to be the absolute lowest point of my existence to date—I could barely see the diagrams on the chalk board, could barely get enough oxygen in order to think, didn't dare cough, the dik was being squashed, mutilated and ruined, especially as Francine bent her soft shoulders to her task, which ought to have been attending to the dik, was my opinion. I could think only of the trajectories of phlegm, mucus and semen that would explode out of me if an impulse to cough or sneeze had really taken hold—I could imagine it—there's this enormous Bang!, so much stuff comes out of me that my head is reduced in size by fifty per cent, wild loops and strings of goo fly through the air like serpentine, the dik succeeds in *levering off* the top of the desk, bellowing, firing and gushing—the trajectory's end, of course, of all this matter, the sexy, undeserving (mostly) and horrified Francine. She who of course *knew* that I was full of crap; she said so all the time.

This event seemed a *inevitable*, because at that age you know that the worst things you can imagine about yourself *are true*, they will come to pass.

Later, at home, having cleansed my eyes, lungs, nose and throat, I set about helping the dik. Its favorite copy of *Life*, the Broadway gamine on page 57 wrapping her legs around that guy. The piston is, of course, not a machine—I suspect it to be an ungodly combination of the wheel and the lever, coupled with the idea of planetary or eccentric gearing.

Discussion of dik issues with Cowznofski, whom I encountered the next day: He approached me in some embarrassment in the locker room and said he had experienced a wet dream the night before, had this happened to me yet? The guy's *yet*, his *certainty*! I felt sorry for Cowznofski though, because I knew his mother to be a ferocious housekeeper. But no, I said, I had to say no, I have not experienced this yet, because, *Cowznofski*, I thought, *I* don't have enough at the end of the day to have a wet dream *with*. And thinking of my piston I went to sit behind Francine in fourth period math.

Our textbook, *Nussbaum's Geometry*, served sometimes to remind me that there were, possibly, alternatives to these Francine tortures. There was a girl called Nussbaum in biology class, thin and dark, who always wore striped stockings. The title of the text gave me to dream the geometry of Nussbaum, her stripy legs in a perfect V. What is that? Ninety degrees?

All this ends—you go to college and get yourself a girl, or don't. But you grow up, don't you? A little? And you leave the sea of mucus far below.

FRICTION COUPLINGS

Things widen, for a time, when you're lucky and young. Much depends upon the lever being applied to an object with the optimal inertia/momentum.

In Terms of Momentum:

① Applying the lever upward to your girl on the rolling stenographic chair in her office results in A) loss of power in the lever if the wheels keep rolling and sufficient force cannot be continuously applied ('You *gotta* give me somewhere to stand,' said Archimedes, 'or I'm gonna look like a fuckin' idiot over here') and B) loss of your girl's job when the executive producer walks in and C) subsequent loss of your girl because of loss B (1973). ② In applying the lever orally, the fulcrum should be inverted by 180 degrees so that the lever matches the curvature of the mouth and throat. The journal and its bearing are then working in proper unison. But this assemblage, though mechanically correct, may result in a loss of A) respect and B) girl, depending on the moral temperature of the working relationship (1979). The lever needs resistance of course to function properly and in some cases the height and firmness of the ordinary kitchen or farmhouse table may provide a mechanically satisfactory basis for leverage and coupling. The support pads of the beloved object may fail in time under pressure of leverage from the edge of the table, however, resulting in A) complaints of wear (= 'pain'), B) complaints of butter and jam markings on clothing and C) loss of object (1981).

In Terms of Inertia:

① Beginning from a crouching position, the lever may be applied to your girl positioned on her grandmother's antique needlepoint footstool, resulting in A) breakage of stupid wooden stool legs and B) lever and mechanic being thrown out (1977). ② The headboard of any ordinary hotel bed can be used by your girl, so *you* opine, as a bracing point, her hands apart, when applying the lever from behind in a mutually kneeling position. This is mechanically excellent. If the headboard is not affixed firmly to the wall, however, subsequent motions will result in wasted, 'collateral' torques causing A) violent vibration and partial destruction of headboard, and B) mechanic *and* object to be thrown out of hotel and left to argue bitterly, wandering all night through the streets of Charleston, South Carolina (1986).

In Terms of Mechanically Complex Arrangements of Inertia and Momentum:

① A 'springy' lever may be applied between the mammary assemblages, where one may enjoy in pleasant fashion a demonstration of Newtonian principles of action and reaction. If this is OK. If not, there maybe a significant loss of A) energy and B) all contact. Even by phone (1982). ② A 'springy' lever may be applied with its fulcrum at the apex of your *new* girl, the two bodies conjoined as with a mitre tongued and grooved, the pleasant sensations being produced akin to those experienced when an ordinary metal spatula is inserted under an ordinary wheaten pancake on any domestic iron griddle—and giving rise to memories of such pancakes—which may result in a loss of concentration and an early decoupling, it being impossible in most circumstances winningly to say 'Gonna flip you like a flapjack' (1974). ③ The wearing of shoes by your girl which incorporate principles of the wedge and/or inclined plane—there is debate over which may be an application of the other—in any case the *sister machines of the lever*—cannot be urged more strongly. One of the most satisfactory, mechanically classical linkages is easily achieved in this manner, in a standing position against an ordinary wall (forget headboards). The mechanism produced is a complex though highly successful combination of inertias and momentums, each infinitely controllable at any moment by both operators, the necessary angles and pressures involved quite variable. (*See* R. Siffredi, *Opera*).

Discussion of dik issues with Hartley Backus, my employer in the fine arts business where I worked after college, hoping to avoid most of life by being taken into a family firm: Mr Backus dealt in expensive paintings and glassware, had been interested in them from an early age, and financed his own collecting with the profits from his family's vocation, the breeding of cattle. The atmosphere in our offices was schizophrenic. Mr Backus had a large bull made of turquoise Murano glass on his desk, a desk in which, I happened to know, he stored adult magazines along with auction reports on paintings, objets d'art and cows. He was a kindly man, tall and hale, gruff about most things, and despite being married to a flighty and bovine society matron who gave all her time to the Board of the Zoo, I knew he took a general interest in genital issues. He approached my desk in some embarrassment and excitement one day, with a large painting tied up in brown paper. 'Take a look at this,' he said, 'just got it from Parke-Bernet.' He cut the string with the frightening miniature surgical scissors he always kept in his pocket, scissors with which you might perform a vasectomy. He carefully took off the paper. The painting proved to be one of the hundreds of thousands of nineteenth-century oils of prize bulls, probably English— the English painted their cows before their families, their castles, or even themselves. The prize bull was standing, proud and irritated, in a field of grass and flowers, some trees and out-buildings in the background. With his large, graceful hand, Mr Backus made an affectionate, cupping gesture at the bull's testicles. 'Would you look at that?' he said. 'What a sack of nuts.' With his finger he traced along the thing's thirty-inch dik. 'Look at that,' he said. '*ZING!*'

THEY HAVE THEIR SAY

1. *'You're very large. But when TIM had an erection, he really had an erection.'*

TIM? What a thing to say, and just when you thought things were going so well. And hadn't she *dumped* Tim? Not in favor of you, you weren't on the scene yet. So what was all this yearning for the dik of Tim, someone you thought of as existing in a mental ash can along with his camper van, the only thing you knew about him, rather now the only *other* thing you knew about him. So he got a really firm, but tiny, *camper boner.* Big deal.

2. *'It's the penis of a* man.'

Well, yes, you thought, it is, obviously. But then—what? What do you mean? Do you mean it has somehow been stuck on to someone who is not a man? Do you mean it looks like it belongs to some other man? *Who?*

3. *'Do you know you have a beautiful cock?'*

she wrote, at the beginning of what was to be a short-lived epistolary and telephonic affair. Wait a minute: aside from your first weekend together, you only met up in person once more, in *Philadelphia,* the well known anti-erotic place on the eastern seaboard. You had never received a letter like this, had you? In truth you got little mail. Your clearest memory of this whole shenanigan is of standing half naked in your bathroom in dim afternoon light, the telephone wedged against your ear, the lever springing about, desperate for an object, desperate for her, as she lay on some padded inclined plane in Philadelphia, and whispered.

4. *'What are you* doing?'

she said, when it was pretty plain. But you felt insulted, didn't you? Because what you were doing you were doing for the second time 'in a row', that is to say almost imme-diately, and this it must be said was not often part of your schematic. This incensed you, this return of the king, and her comment on it while bent over the sofa, so like an idiot you had to have it out with her, demand that she acknowledge that when you gave, you gave your *all*. And that it was pretty damned wonderful.

5. *'Just release the hose and everything will be fine,'*

she actually said there in the greenhouse in Sicily. And ba-dum-bump the inner vaudevillean said, *And how many times have I heard THAT before?* But her words had the blessed and almost magical effect of releasing the hose, the invisible restraining latch, L, letting go, yes *letting go* of its pain or whatever is bothering it all the time; the hose unwound, the old *tubo* became the lever and plunged into her green fork there like a stalk of the meatiest vegetable, *rabarbaro* or *asparagi* . . . all those nineteenth-century cartoons of elegant women in the cafés, eating thick asparagus, holding the shafts delicately—they play at it being half way down their throats, or they just kiss the speary, lemony tip with their pretty lips—the goateed *roués* looking around in knowing delight from other tables . . .

6. *'When we first met, I thought you were really—'*

and here she drew her index fingers apart, which made you think:

ZING!

But then in the car, on the way to the supermarket, you thought: What does she mean, when we *first* met? What the hell has changed? Nothing has changed! And when you changed the gear lever, you looked down there. People should choose their words carefully.

No! No! You were not deficient! Proof: the length, L, from your belt, B, to the spot, S, on your hideous maroon double-knit trousers of 1972, which appeared as your girl kissed you in the Roy and Niuta Titus Auditorium. When the lights came up the old lady in front of you asked, rather *pointedly*, if you had enjoyed the show, *On the Avenue* with Madeleine Carroll and the Ritz Brothers. Sure.

When you came out into 53rd Street and the sun, your girl said, *You've got a spot.* The spot persisted through the West Fifties, eventually drying out on Amsterdam Avenue, A.

LISA'S STUFFED TAIL

I left Mr Backus's employ because I was never going to join the family firm; there's no way you're going to lever yourself into that, I said to myself. Besides, his only daughter was too tall and easily disgusted.

My next job was as floor manager for a small television station dedicated to the public good; it still transmitted in black and white. One day I was surprised to see an acquaintance of mine show up at our tiny studios; she was in a nascent theater/dance group who were to perform on the air as part of the station's commitment to the 'community', whatever that meant—at any rate it's an idea long gone from America. They'd 'devised' (Mr and Mrs Theatergoer, *always* dread this word) a show about animals, their 'personalities', with *painfully slow movements* designed to show . . . something . . . and a deeply self-deceived narration—importance of the forests, so on. They had made some good-looking costumes, thank god for that, said the director, who was wondering why life had led him to this, making a program of slow-moving animals in black and white at the age of thirty. The woman I knew, Lisa, was supposed to be a sort of small Malaysian honeybear, which, I found out later, having been sexually stimulated to look it up, looks adorable but is ferocious in the extreme. Lisa was stitched into a tight-fitting romper of brown velour, complete with ears and a thick, long tail stuffed with foam rubber; the tail was almost the same volume as one of her legs.

This was a dreary day, I remember it as almost unending—the piece was over two hours long and there was to be a rehearsal first. The director had only two cameras to work with, two *black and white cameras*, and could barely bring himself to map out the shots with his assistant. My job was simply to *endure*, standing between the two cameras and listlessly pointing from one to the other (we had no tally lights), as if it mattered—the actor/dancers had never been on television and most of them couldn't see out of their masks and rubber heads. The cameramen Harvey and Stan and I fortified ourselves with dope and with baloney sandwiches from across the street.

The rehearsal went badly, stopping and starting. Stan was listening to the ball game the whole time—something he'd rigged up in his headphones. We had a break and the actors, including Lisa, sat around in a circle on the floor, drinking mineral water and eating organic snacks, these *gritty treats*, talking about their roles. Lisa was pretty and I saw Harvey taking notice of this on his way to and from the alley for his top-up joint.

'Roll tape,' the director sighed, and the whole miserable thing began again, perhaps after all with more verve than before. You should have heard the music. The cameras clicked on and off and I pointed, sometimes, mechanically, from 1 to 2 . . . gazing up into the lighting grid and noticing that No. 18 Flood wasn't screwed on properly . . . I could see in my monitor that Harvey's pans were getting swoony . . . the sinsemilla . . . but what the hell, he was *adding movement*. 'I like it, Harvey,' the director said in our headphones. 'Keep doing that.'

Now came Lisa's close-ups—she was supposed to slowly go down on her knees, and then flat out on the floor. Maybe it was hibernation. She moved well, I thought. I was only used to seeing her serve coffee in a bistro near my place. She had a gaunt New Age boyfriend whom you couldn't imagine inspiring any sensual movement—or this was the opinion of the men in the bistro. As Lisa lay back she neatly adjusted her tail so that it rested between her legs. Harvey was supposed to zoom in slowly on her lowered metabolic rate. But I became aware of a breathier noise, a *wheezing*, and the zoom wasn't happening. I looked away from the monitor and found that Harvey had *left his camera* and was standing over Lisa, looking down at her, staring at her rich thick tail, which did look now like a big brown furry dik stuffed between her velour thighs. Harvey's eyes were popping out of his head and he was wheezing, utterly fascinated by this plush member; he was poised to invade Lisa, fuck the honeybear, and he had a hard-on, risibly visible through his dumb-looking combat trousers. And then I realized that I'd got one too, from Lisa's thighs, the texture of the velour, and from knowing her a little.

Harvey looked over at my thing and down at his, then at Lisa's closed eyes, her pretty lips and her low metabolic rate. He was in agony. The dik was in agony and even Stan was watching now. 'So,' Harvey said. 'Here it is. Right here at work. Totem and taboo. Jesus Christ, look at that.' Stan shifted his gaze to *my* trousers. *Cincinnati seven, San Francisco six, the bases loaded* buzzed the headphones. 'Harvey?' said the director. 'Harvey? Hell. Stop tape.'

La Piazza del Floppolo

We have all sat in the Piazza, *gentiluomini*, protest though you may. Most days we pass it on the bus, giving it as little thought as a Roman does the Forum or a New Yorker his Chrysler Building—*something from the past, yes*; or we think of it as a baroque, peaceful place where one day we'll sit alone with our memories, feeding seed to pigeons. The truth is we find ourselves here with regularity, at times of sorrow, of crisis, or at times of wine.

The Piazza has an essentially Venetian character— Venice on a chilly, dripping night, when it's impossible to conceive why this terrain was settled or why anyone would persist in living in it. The restaurants are closed, the buildings look like things made by other animals, not compassionate men and women, and for you especially gaiety has gone far away.

Your bench is hard. You have no money, and after having *failed*, it always rains.

Fuck me, baby. The real surprise of hearing an *actual* human being say this—especially when you were engaged in said activity. This led to extreme self-doubt; suddenly you were looking down on the both of you, not as from heaven but from about eight feet up. The whole thing became a frightening cartoon, including the character of her roughly-shaven long-term squeeze, who was at that moment in *prison*, and you shut up your little shop and headed for the Piazza as quickly and predictably as one collects two hundred dollars in Monopoly.

The Piazza contains a noted *obelisk*, stolen from an earlier and more vigorous civilization, painstakingly levered into an upright position here. At night it is dimly lit, and sitting around with the others, you RUE it. You're *supposed* to rue it. Birds sit on it during the day and make it look ridiculous.

Let's! I always liked to—with you. Well here was another *rude surprise*, having just stopped at her place for a drink. Not having 'been there' for a period of months. Suddenly here was the shade being lowered, the lights being lowered, the shag carpet, freshly shampooed with bemused nostalgia it seemed. Here was a second drink and her reappearance in some things which really had inflamed you, those months before. All right? Well—no!?, ye gods, and because she's still friendly and still eager and therefore you suppose still your *friend*, you feel that a frank confession of your lonely and frantic habits since you stopped seeing her will explain things if not exactly set them to rights. Where were the energies of that very afternoon? God damn it?

In the Piazza del Floppolo no one does anything. They sit around on the stone benches and they brood on their opportunities, lost and to come, and they drink. Sometimes wine has landed them in the Piazza; once in a while wine will get them out of it. But many of them drink too much, and in their brooding they simultaneously assign greater *and* lesser loves, values, and meanings to those objects they meant to lever and more. In a niche of the south wall of the Piazza (*c.*1570) there is a small bust of Archimedes.

You'd been struggling to love in winter, the two of you, or rather YOU had been struggling to love. Why do there have to be so many differing ideas, reactions to the same stimuli? You would think that the weekend by yourselves in the pretty farmhouse, the snow, the trees, the *cardinals* would state all that needed to be stated. If not, then the simple act of *warming up*, after all that, would cause a physical change, a simple chemical reaction that would *remind* both bodies, both heads, that there was business to be done. What are snow and cardinals *for*? And perhaps she had been merely, simply, prettily reacting to these stimuli and so had you, because look at that thing wedged into your pants, but you *also* had been trying to lever *love* into the situation, the snow and the trees. Out of the cardinal pair into the two of you.

So far the weekend had been perhaps *too* snowy, and cardinaled. There were two different libidos and libidinous ideas when you arrived in the pretty farmhouse kitchen, with its simple farmhouse table, after your walk, stamping the snow off your boots and hanging up your scarves. You were not without a sense of the sexually dramatic, and were going to suggest a bout on the simple farmhouse table, because you thought she would like it but mostly because you were *forcing yourself to love her*, so that simple farmhouse tablefucking would be OK. You wanted to love her and be in her right away. Just at this moment, she came out with *her* libido blazing and said, before cocoa had even been *mentioned*—

How about you come in my mouth? and this was so outrageous and unfair, wasn't it, because she was making a *more vivid* suggestion than *you* had worked up, she was suggesting something purely sexual right there in the pretty farmhouse kitchen! Something singularly sexual which would not involve gazing into each others' eyes or ultimately, in the broad sense, going upstairs and *snuggling* beneath the traditional farmhouse quilt, for ever and ever. But here—who knows?—she might even have made this outrageous suggestion because of a real love for you! That she had conceived in the snow and because of the trees! And the cardinals!

The idea of the Piazza and your hard stone seat in it

became complex, at this disappointing moment, became *Cubist*, because the night before she'd given you the biggest dik you'd ever had—it *ripped the elastic*—and it had felt as if *all* your bones had entered her, lovable, and so sweet.

One of the games you can play, with yourself of course, to pass the time in the Piazza del Floppolo, and you may see the other gents doing it too, is making up new names for it, which might amuse or even inspire, stimulate the damned thing to action. *Pecorino, pecorella* (amusing). *My big bologn'* (stimulating).

Er . . . do you want to wait? she said, having intended, started even, to give you a blowjob in the cemetery. Well? What *was* the problem? She had blonde hair, nails a startling red in the sun, and very useful lips, which you had already tasted on your putatively innocent stroll. Was it that you suddenly looked around and realized you were in a cemetery? Or was it that she was married?

In the middle of a sinsemilla-filled summer, he says to his girlfriend, Let's do a lot of sexy stuff but *not fuck*. But what does he have in mind? Finding a fancy fulcrum; she standing on the lever; he'd use it as a whisk? He thought she'd find this fun, because she *was* fun. He meant of course there'd be so much more leverage, so much more sound and foam, the next time. (It's true that after the tide goes out, all is lost; the beach becomes empty and windswept.) But she doesn't get it. She demands the works or nothing! As is her right.

His own dik was made to *retract*, for cultural and parental reasons, as I keep explaining to you . . .

In the Piazza del Floppolo are reminders of many wars. Wars we have caused, *gentiluomini*, all our wars which will never end. It's particularly depressing, on your hard bench in the chilly, dripping night, to see that exedra, bristling with silent eighteenth-century cannons, all pointing *slightly* upward, but not upward enough, you think ruefully. And you rue the succeeding thought, all those diks mounted on spoked wheels in the eighteenth century; in Rops, in Ungerer. Why don't the women stop war? Is it really, one is given to ruefully thinking in the Piazza, because if the women intervened in our wars, in our stupid man-shit, that we'd go crazy and flop, denying them the dik, possibly forever? Lowering our cannons would do that? They'd flop, we'd flop, as if we, our diks were made by Dali and not Krupp?

Thought you were all fixed, didn't you? Thought this was really the one. Because mutual background. Because you middle-aged lonely fool. Because red hair. Because she said, almost every day, *You're big!* And that in turn made it so—until, a mere week after you were 'officially' together, seemingly accepted by her family, and she by yours (no mean achievement), you unexpectedly found yourself sitting in an *abject* position during a little party she gave. The bamboo and foam rubber imitation sofa you were sitting on *forced you into an abject position*: low to the ground, knees squeezed together, hunched forward—it couldn't be helped, you were obliged to talk to her aunt—nor could you avoid the famous thoughts of damage to seminal vesicles from foam rubber . . . The moment you said to yourself, *Hey, I'm sitting in an abject position*, saw that everyone was looking down on you, you saw her, saw the way she was standing talking to her sister's husband, a large, impossibly nice guy. She was standing directly in front of him, near the fire, a drink in one hand and cupping her elbow with the other, *beaming* up at him as he *beamed* down at her. She was nodding vigorously. Had she ever agreed with *you* so strongly? She was standing with her legs apart, in her long Pre-Thanksgiving Mood skirt, in her dead-leaf colored shoes. (All this bland understatement, it should have *told* you.) Her stance was weird and made you uncomfortable. Later as she passed him on the way to the kitchen, you saw her touch his *lower back*, which is not a place you . . . How could you possibly have put up with this? Are you an idiot? Yet you did put it out of your mind for many months of your foolish liaison, but it colored and devascularized many things from that moment. You on your little divan of abjection, off which you couldn't gracefully lever yourself. Everyone looking.

The overriding feeling of being male is that of being empty. Particularly when the Fates have sent you to the Piazza for a while. It is empty even if there are other men there, you're all empty because of the little thing being a little thing at the inopportune moment.

There are other plazas of failure in the world, squares

of questioning. You could be having the same thoughts in the Place Pigalle, having failed to find a lover to pay; you could be in Times Square, in the back of a police car.

Don't the girls know it's all brinksmanship, the lever? That there is only emptiness wrapped in doubt inside? That the *Hindenburg* looked rigid but wasn't? It was just full of *gas*, you think on your cold bench in the Piazza. What *about* Archimedes and his infuriating qualification? Fucking crybaby.

What you always end up thinking, what each man thinks on his drizzly chilly nights in the Piazza is: will it ever allow me to lever myself out of my quandary?

It's cold and drippy in the Piazza. In another part of the city, seemingly inaccessible on a night like tonight, there are bands playing, there are fireworks, and men chase masked girls through increasingly narrow *vicoli*.

Rocco

Let's run it up the flagpole and see who salutes it, as they used to say on Madison Avenue, in their Bermuda shorts, in their all-male bars. But how many men have seen other men being men? We hide it from *women* as much as we can, and we absolutely hide it from each other. We lever brothers, we little freemasons of the dik!

He has a friend with an enormously complicated, even dangerous, amorous life. Women having to be pried out of bed, urged down back stairs, as the next rings at the front door, another circling overhead in an airplane . . . He thinks of his friend's life as the front of a cathedral, full of tiny boxed scenes, all of them richly stimulating and full of real drama, or at least skilful melodrama. So he asks him, in the changing room, out of the scientific curiosity we little freemasons all affect from time to time, has he ever seen another guy's hard-on? *In person?* And Joe Cathedral, who likes being admired and likes to think of himself as, or act as, an open book on these issues, be-comes guarded, cagey and sly—to the astonishment of his questioner. The whole thing takes quite a bit of time, and long after they have left the changing room and left the usual coffee shop and the guy who asked *a simple question* is sitting in his own kitchen, all he's been given is the shadow of a possibility that Joe and a college roommate once enjoyed their respective girlfriends together, so there might have been something. Or maybe that was some-body else. And there was a weekend in Las Vegas which involved two men and one prostitute and that really prob-ably was almost definitely someone else.

What's the big secret? If Joe could look at the guy's girl, naked and so on, why can't he look at the guy? Did he really *not look*?

Walking by the reflecting pool in the museum, talking of girls and not *Holbein* like the guards think you're sup-posed to, he was astonished by his other friend, the tall one with the *wife and daughter*, who earnestly sat down on the stone surrounding the reflecting pool, like you're not supposed to, and announced, not at the lowest volume, that when he rents videotapes he rents gay videotapes; all stick and no carrot. So he asked the tall friend why, as one of the guards sidled casually over, and the tall guy said, Well, I'm straight, see? Married. So I know *all about that*. I know where this goes, and that goes. At *home*. So I wanna see how the other guys do it.

The other guys—that was a sweet way of putting it, wasn't it? So the tall friend sat around occasionally with a beer, in a positive forest of dik!

ZING!

He didn't want to ask him about any personal dik experiences, as the guard had come over to listen, and the tall friend had been privately educated.

We hide it from each other, we freemasons of the dik. In our little aprons and our little lodges with no windows. Nobody's seen it, hah?

BUT THERE IS ONE PLACE WE MAY SEE IT, GENTIL-UOMINI, and that is mounted on the guaranteed non-retracting pylon of Rocco Siffredi.

Rocco is our mascot; a tribune of the people. It hardly needs mentioning, but it is extremely unfortunate that this unselfish person, this *living testament* to what everyone wants and needs, is perforce hidden away in a reviled subterranean world.

Rocco has restored the lever to its rightful place in society. Or at least he's trying. If we would only let him!

Rocco is much better for us than Star Wars, or *Tolkien*, because he really exists. He lives and loves for all! We masonic, cowardly dik-hiders! A LIBERATOR. He's our little scoutmaster, though my wife says that sounds unsavoury.

One is reminded of the painting in the House of the Vetti in Pompeii, of Priapus putting his putz on a pair of scales, looking with pride and distress at his enormous dik.

Rocco has demonstrated, it goes without saying, that the Roman catapult can still be effective. Especially when he's having a springy day. Remember the two girls in Amsterdam? He shows us often how to power the lever by applying it almost vertically—the effectiveness of this was obvious: it seemed the girl on all fours might suddenly fly off the bed, or even out the window. And when the other girl got semen in her eye, Rocco was right there with a towel, *che gentiluomo*. After all, mechanisms have to be tended. Have you ever been to a macaroni factory? There are a lot of handsome men standing around with damp cloths.

Cf. the countless old engravings of tiny women joyfully sliding down giant diks; something from the seaside funhouse of the unconscious.

The mortise joint Rocco formed with the London girl—levering them both into a geometric pattern, a theorem!, something straight out of *Nussbaum's*—her acute angle—for our pleasure! Or, with Agnes on the marble-topped table—a perfect bit of mechanics—she was one of the ones who fall in love with him after a mere hour of leverage, and to this the lever responds enthusiastically (as we all know). And later she reached under the little padded bench and worked the lever herself. And with Kati, working on her, as if she were a beautiful long white piece of Travertine, the dik like a strong cable in a quarry.

Rocco has demonstrated that you can lever your balls, B, into your beloved object, O (the will, W, on both sides must be strong). But as Stephenson, he of the *Rocket*, said, 'There is no limit to the speed if the works can be made to stand.'

But Rocco's most important discovery is of course that of the Archimedes Position, levering from behind, she on all fours, Rocco (or you!) up on his feet—this is mechanically brilliant, as it ensures a steady object and an angle of wonder, for both parties—AND: it is *most indisputably mammalian*. Rocco stepped in for us, lads, and, enacting the guy's theories, offered the firm, willing dik of eternal male friendship to Archimedes himself.

Never let it be said that there are not salient warnings, *cogent warnings* for Rocco in the sober disciplines of History and Science. Particularly apt is this passage from one of the better-known works on mechanics:

Impact—or collision—is a pressure of short duration between two bodies. Unless there is some special reason for using impact in machines, it ought to be avoided, on account not only of the waste of energy which it causes, but from the damage it occasions to the frame and mechanism.

Rocco is a man of action, a Machiavelli, a da Vinci. Even if he were to disappear tomorrow, Rocco has left behind much wisdom that we, fellows, should bind to our hearts, as lovingly as if they were the Quotations of Mao. We should ponder his pensées on penises, and the human condition, all our lives.

> *That the most down you can go?*
> *Go maximum down.*
> *Put in, baby. Put in.*
> *More. More more your ass.*

ROCCO'S GUIDE TO WESTERN ART

Scene 1. Ext. Fountain of Trevi day. Rocco lounges naked in the water, his great schlong draped across Nettuno's thighs. Tourists are throwing coins and jeering.

ROCCO: (*To camera.*) Hello there, this Rocco. Welcome my guida Western Art. This Fountain of Trevi, really great fountain. This show where water, really important for human race, come to Roma, and it was a virgo who show the guys the exact spot, so there's a beautiful statua of that virgo.

This one of my favorite spot in the whole world because I'm here with Nettuno, my home boy, Italian like me, and these girls here Health and Fertility, which all good stuff I think and I believe in. I also like this fontana because 'Trevi' mean 'three way' so I believe in this too. (*Coins hit him in the face.*)

Cut to:

Scene 2. Ext. day. Rocco in his usual natty trousers, sport shirt, giacca and sunglasses in a Roman park of note. It could be the gardens of the Palatine, or along the Via Appia Antica—anywhere that is choked with broken statuary. There should be a panorama of the hills and domes of Rome in the background.

ROCCO: All the time people ask me. They come to Roma—beautiful città—for to understand history of art. And they look around and they ask me: *Rocco, where all the dik?* So I decide to find out for myself.

Pan across broken statuary.

ROCCO: Somebody must have got very mad, at some point, and knock all the dik off the statue. But who. And why. If you don't have the dik sometime, then the art is not about human race. Then is not art. Is my theory.

A girl walks into shot, badly acting the 'innocent tourist'. Rocco puts his arm around her and they walk out of frame together. Zoom in on skyline. Dissolve to:

Scene 3. Int. Baths of Diocletian day. Rocco and the girl, arms entwined, enter a large domed gallery. At the top is an oculus. Rocco looks skeptically at a range of herms—heads and busts mounted on tapered pedestals. Rocco and the girl walk up and down, inspecting the herms. Bad acting of looking interested. Rocco stops, turns to camera.

ROCCO (*pointing*): See, I don't like this. Here they get
    away with no body. Like they took away whole
    body. Why you have to hide the dik? Why you have
    to hide the body? Look these guys. (*To the girl.*) You
    like this?

GIRL: No, I don't like.

ROCCO (*to camera*): See? Like women don't like the dik?
    You got to be kidding me.

*Rocco and the girl exit. As Rocco passes a statue of Aphrodite he
gently puts his hand on her breast.*

ROCCO: You're the best, baby.

Dissolve to:

*Scene 4. Ext. Piazza del Poppolo day. A large, open piazza
with many fountains and Egyptian obelisks. Pan across piazza,
taking in fountains, girls, ending on Rocco, framed between two
of the obelisks. The girl is on his arm, idly, discreetly squeezing
his crotch.*

ROCCO: (*to camera, after looking over his shoulder.*) See, this
    what happen when you hide the dik. You get *obelisk.*
    (*Waves contemptuously.*) You go to other country and
    you get big FAKE dik. Then you bring to your
    country and stick it up, meanwhile less and less real
    dik and everyone thinking: *WHAT?* Is not fair.

Close-up on the (Roman-added) metallic 'sunburst' on top of one of the obelisks.

ROCCO: What *this* supposed to be? Big come? You see, no dik, everything become fake. It's what I think.

Cut to:

Scene 5. Int. Vatican City day. Crane shot: pan down across crowd in the Sistine Chapel to discover Rocco lying on the floor, with the girl. He is still wearing his sunglasses; she is blowing him. Hold. Rocco finally takes his sunglasses off. Keeps concentrating. Hold. Cut to static shot of Michelangelo's God and Adam.

ROCCO (*voice over*): (*Sighs.*) See, something very wrong. I know, Michelangelo, great painter, really great Italian artist. But look at the dik! *What* going on with this dik? This supposed to be Adamo, right? The guy who start whole human race? With this? There six thousand people here and I bet nobody believe it. No wonder you got to rent binocular.

Cut to:

Scene 6. Int. gallery day. Rocco is standing somewhat overfamiliarly with the 'Trastevere' Hercules Epitrapèzios. The girl hangs on it admiringly.

ROCCO (*to camera, confidentially*): After looking all over Roma, I finally found a guy with hard-on. This

Hercules, really strong guy, also defeated a lot of Amazons. (*The girl purrs.*) *This* the kind of guy we need. Look at this. This what art supposed to be. Way to love, big guy!

Rocco and the girl walk out of the gallery.

GIRL: Ciao! Ciao, Ercole!

Rocco exists; think about it. What is it like to *be Rocco?* To imagine, one can only use one's own lever, which responds to Rocco like a moth's antenna.

There's no point in trying, from our position, to debate his moral and financial relationships with his employees, partners, clients. Rocco is married with a family, so he can't escape problems, no one can: has he gloomy thoughts in the shower, has he to *drive to work*? But, for us, in his company the Piazza del Floppolo recedes, across the sea. It dies, like Atlantis.

But we are all mortal. *Rocco is mortal.* So we will not think about what will happen to Rocco when the dik no longer works. Let's face it, the best way to proceed is as the Soviets did, with *no clear line of succession.* That's the male thing to do.

WHEEL

*An eccentric may be made capable of having its eccentricity
altered by means of an adjusting screw, so as to vary the extent
of the reciprocating motion which it communicates.*

I am only twenty-five, thought Federico, whose real name
was Roderick, so it doesn't matter what I do for a living. He hated the name Roderick, hated even more being
called *Rod*, which he thought alarmed people sexually—
they would put him in Russ Meyer movies of the mind.
So Sidney had made him the gift of his new name, on his
last birthday.

It's a lot like Roderick, said Sidney, but literally much
more sympathetic. You'll see. It'll work great for you.

It was stupid to think the way Federico was thinking
about his life. First of all, life, even in America, where
everybody is on a continual and monstrous diet of distraction, can be very short. Federico was aware of this at
times. Two hundred years ago, he thought, I would be
at the peak of my profession. Whatever it was. And five
hundred years ago, I'd be dead! Ho ho!

Second, Federico was living in a city where almost every other person thought it *was very important* what you did for a living. It was extremely important at the age of twenty-five, as you would have finished your degree and of course would know exactly what you should do, would know *what needed to be done*. But these types had also known at the age of eighteen. And at twelve. And when they were four, deciding on their universities.

But because he had been raised kindly but blindly, Federico believed in a sort of playground existing before one settled down. He believed that the right profession would *find him*, because he believed himself more or less capable of anything—with application. He didn't mind that this already ruled out the law, medicine, college professorships or being an astronaut.

Federico's situation was simple. He worked at *Variety*, founded in 1905 by SIME SILVERMAN, as a page editor and reviewer. The job was easy and usually enjoyable—and he liked to think that it was *allied* to other talents he had, for which he would one day be recognized. As he witnessed hundreds of bad plays and motion pictures a year, he felt sure that one day he would write a better one. He had innate, though dormant, beliefs in himself as a director and even as an actor. But week by week, month by month all he pretty much did was go by subway to the office every morning, and drink beer at night with his colleagues or friends.

Federico had a small, very neat apartment on the West Side, *fairly* near the Park, and down the street from him lived his girlfriend, who also had a small, neat apartment.

The whole arrangement was very small and neat, perhaps too much so. Initially Federico had been full of joy when his girlfriend decided to move onto his street. He thought it must mean that she loved him.

How small and neat would that be? In the city that is never small and never neat.

Federico's girlfriend worked on Wall Street, doing something she didn't understand. Federico understood: she was a sell-out. But he told himself that it didn't matter what she did for a living because she was only twenty-three.

They rotated between each other's apartments, sometimes staying the night and sometimes not. Federico preferred his girlfriend's apartment on a hot night, as she had bigger windows and got more of a breeze from the street. He associated her bamboo window shades with the dope she smoked. However, he thought his apartment was quieter, more private, a better place for their kookier exploits.

We don't like each other much, Federico told himself almost every morning on the subway. But this fucking is very interesting, so it doesn't matter because I'm only twenty-five and she's only twenty-three. He liked thinking about fucking her when he was on the subway.

She had all these poses. She was a tremendous *poseuse*, he thought, and hoped to be able to use the phrase in one of his reviews. (She almost never accompanied him to the theater; she always fell asleep. Even during *Mark Twain Tonight!*, which he'd paid for.) She was a kind of freaky homebody, who liked staying in with her tapes and her marijuana. She worshiped her family, who all thought she was weird. And a sell-out.

Her primary pose was one of 'innocence'. This obtained throughout the levels of her existence, meaning she acted innocent at work—they all did, even though they were ripping everybody off; to her family she acted as though she never drank or smoked or even slept with Federico.

He got the feeling that they watched this performance with some incredulity. Her mother was no idiot. Her father was sort of an idiot, but that might have been overwork.

This innocent act was pervasive. It was probably obsessional, but who knows about any of that when you're twenty-five?

In bed, Federico was made to feel, to act, as if he was invading her innocence, depriving her of it. It was better when they were at his place, with regard to the neighbors, and the municipal rules about noise, because sometimes she would get up and run around and around the apartment, demanding that he capture and deflower her.

There was also a scenario where Federico would paint her toenails while she drank Schlitz and dallied with his cock in her mouth; they would then go to the bedroom, which she had emptied of everything save the bed, a large number of pillows, and a heavy black leather belt, which she'd bought in the Village.

There were nights when Federico had to wait outside her bedroom, until he heard the little dramatic sounds, when he was to enter, surprise her in *the act of self-pollution*, and chastise her.

Then there were the nights when Federico's girlfriend's girlfriend joined them. She was as voluptuous as she was vacuous; her only conversation consisted in saying over and over again that her grand-uncle sat on the Supreme Court. They didn't seem to have much contact, unless she was making the Justice's ears burn in Washington as she endlessly babbled about him while being licked by Federico's girlfriend and rammed by Federico in New York. The northeast corridor. This girl, thought Federico, looked like the old-fashioned KILLER BARBIE, before Barbie became a cheerleader and then the perpetual victim of cookie-buying pedophiles: her stripy swimsuit, swept-up hair smelling of Kent cigarettes, her fuck-me-or-go-to-hell eyes, killer legs, killer mules, killer TITS.

So it was all very New York, perhaps especially with the poses of innocence. Federico didn't feel particularly innocent or guilty. He merely felt that he was where he ought to be in life at the age of twenty-five: surviving, enjoying himself, but not doing too much, not working his ass off like those thirty-year-olds up ahead.

Federico always wanted everything to *continue*, the way he liked it, and hadn't a hope in hell of realizing this wasn't natural, and that even if it *were* natural it'd never have been permitted in New York. Federico was proud of surviving, rather than pillaging, was pleased to be feeding himself and his girlfriend. But doing essentially nothing gets dull, and if you *really* are doing nothing people begin to suspect you.

Although Federico's girlfriend showed no sign of advancing in her job, which was perfectly all right with him at the moment, she of course had her own plans, like anybody. In fact she didn't care what she was doing either, but she had recently decided she loved Federico, or loved him well enough, and that they had a tolerable future. This is what she thought, while he had been thinking that in the end she'd go off with someone else who was on the 'track' he believed her to be on. So things revolve.

A lack of focus set in. Federico would still chase her around whichever apartment they were in, but with increasing feelings of detachment. She sensed this and began a new series of poses and dissimulations. One evening when they were lying in bed, she turned to Federico and told him that her old boyfriend, *Don*, had phoned her. Oh, said Federico. He's working in *Washington*, she said, with the peculiar breathiness that some people reserve for the pronunciation of this awful word—people who suck, people who are idiots. He said he just called to tell me, she said lying there, that he always thought I looked innocent. *Very innocent.*

This was supposed to give Federico a BONER, but he was fast asleep.

And by the way, how fucking believable is it that someone working in *Washington* would find himself musing on *innocence*?

A week later—it was too transparent—she had been out drinking with Killer Barbie. Federico heard the taxi outside, the girls saying good night . . . A minute later she came in and made a huge, affected production of having been approached by some *guy* in the *bar*, he wouldn't let her *alone*, she thought he was going to follow her *home*, blah blah. All the while batting her eyelashes, if you can believe it. Federico said, *I suppose it was your profound air of innocence*, when the telephone rang. She picked it up and made a huge, affected production of It Being the Stranger from the Bar, *No, no, don't call me here, I don't want to see you, stop pursuing me*—when Federico could see full well that it was Killer Barbie on the phone, by pre-arrangement. She ended her act, rolled a joint and looked at him. If you didn't like the guy, said Federico, why'd you give him your phone number? She stared at him for a second and then came up with this: I trusted him initially. Federico said nothing and made no move. She stamped off to bed.

Federico's girlfriend went away for a week, to a conference, from which she issued a barrage of postcards pulsating with dark hints that the men there, all beef-fed, were after her, rubbing up against her and smacking her toosh with their rolled-up conference programs at every opportunity.

Federico used the week to visit some bars on the East Side which he had neglected, and to see Sidney, who was living with his mother on Madison Avenue. They met at their soup and challah place. The guy who ran it was a famous sarcastic. I don't know, my mother's driving me crazy, said Sidney. Literally. She's in the bathroom all morning and the whole house smells like shit and cigarette smoke—they entwine, invariably, immutably, did you know that? Listen, Leo, he said to the sarcastic, is the bathroom available? Sure, Sidney, said Leo—mention my name, you'll get a good seat.

When he came back, Sidney said: You're looking pretty

dapper tonight. What say we go to some totally awful stewardess-type Mexican place and pick us up some? You know—frozen Margaritas till you can't feel your cock or your teeth, and then on with the show.

Maybe a stockbroker, said Federico. I'd like one of them. (Forgetting he had one.) He liked girls who affected suits in their work. Sure—a vulgar, violent evening. What's wrong with that?

The place was as usual—hideous yellow paint, lots of misspelled Spanish words in neon on the walls, bubbly, soupy salsa at the bar which seemed like it contained a *lot* of spit. *Oxcart wheels*, where do they get them.

It developed that Sidney had been here before. If we don't get lucky, they have a chocolate-orange cheesecake that's literally *better than sex*, he said. But there were girls at the bar. Sidney always started working with these *incredible* lines, I will not write them down. *Say, my magic watch says you aren't wearing any underwear—oh, it must be an hour fast. I'm not really this tall—I'm sitting on my wallet. Wow—your beauty has actually stilled the voices in my head! I have only three months to live.* In this place, they worked.

Federico always hung back a little. This is Rod, said Sidney, already completely forgetting, introducing him with the buddy buddy arm around. My name's not *Rod*, said Federico (while thinking that Rod was a name that was right for the joint). My name's Federico. Wow, hi Federico, said a nice girl in a suit, with a huge pleasing pink drink, I'm Thea. Federico's kind of formal sounding—mind if I call you Fed?

They do things *so fast* on the East Side.

No, not at all.

Fed? said Sidney under his breath. What would be wrong with *Rico?*

The conversation was just a sizing-up laced with gin and din. Thea was impressed with Fed's status at *Variety*; he listened to her describe her job and realized she didn't understand it.

Sidney had been right on the physiological button. These *freezing* drinks, with hot cheese and meat thrown periodically on top of them, make a frozen planet of your brain. All is stasis, but you sure can go on talking.

Sidney said good night and went off with his girl, Marcie, after *insisting* that they go to her place because his mother would be awake soon and he didn't want Marcie literally to smell the entwined immutables. Good night, *Fed*, he said.

Federico and Thea, with frozen heads, guts and genitals, though still in a modicum of control, found themselves on the subway for the ferry. Federico was determined that this was going to be romantic. Thea was pretty and wore her suit well. The No. 1 train wheeled around the curved platform at South Ferry and they both felt giddy and laughed.

Thea took his arm as they got on the boat; she had that kind of very straight hair which can seem as though it's made of perfume. Federico's cock twitched—although he couldn't feel it.

So here they were on the boat churning out into the bay. The propellers turned, the moon wheeled into view, as they say, but of course it was the boat turning.

Federico looked up at the wheelhouse, where he saw the captain and the pilot. It suddenly struck him that he would like more control in his life, control had heretofore often been absent. To Thea's surprise, which was, though, agreeably noncommittal, he announced: I suppose a lot of people have fallen in love on this boat. On nights like this. It's the *Cornelius G.* (here he hiccupped) *Kolff.*

Much later, they were struggling together on the bed in Thea's apartment back on the East Side. They were struggling first to stay awake, then not to be sick, thirdly to fuck. Each of them would lose first one battle, then another. After a while they smiled at each other and went into the bathroom together. Federico put a towel under Thea's knees, which she seemed to appreciate. She tickled his neck and took his hand as they both leaned into the bowl. She looks rather nice vomiting, he thought, and he wished she had been in this posture when attempting to play, which hadn't come off.

The water circled and circled in the bowl. Somewhere a big turbine, thought Federico, a big wheel, he supposed, was pumping all this water into New York for their benefit. She was very pretty and sweet, he thought, even though she wasn't the type of girl he usually saw, but so what—he was one of many men thinking that night, as they do every night, that there is no problem in crossing any boundary, that any sign can be ignored—the suit, the salsa, the straight hair. She kept smiling at him while being sick, and the more

Federico barfed the nicer she got. Of course he never saw her again, couldn't remember her name, and the restaurant and her apartment, it's like they never existed.

Not 'when he got home', but when he somehow *found* himself at home the next day, there was a postcard from his girlfriend, whom he hadn't called or written:

It's me.

But this was all hunky dory New Yorky. Federico took little note of his girlfriend's sulks. He was trying to concentrate on the spring, and since their street was *fairly* near the Park he started to jog there, in the morning, for which she berated him, to his surprise. He couldn't decide whether this was because it took him away from her an hour earlier, a reason which would have touched him, or because she thought jogging wasn't decadent enough for the way she wanted to live. This was irritating, as he was starting to know that she in fact had a very ordinary future mapped out for herself. And their nocturnal exertions weren't exactly the sort of exercise you can chalk up to Health, including as they did late hours and quite a few drugs.

One night she was doing the dishes, struggling to clean the EGG BEATER, and suddenly wheeled round to face him. How come nothing's going on with us? she said. What do you mean? said Federico, from the depths of *Variety*. I mean you're not satisfying me is what I mean, she said. Well— said Federico. Listen, we're together, right? she said. Approximately, said Federico. Well, I mean, you've got to be excited, she said. You're supposed to want me all the time. But I am excited, said Federico. No you're not, she said. I want you to come home from work and spank me, hard. I want to be spanked and I want to be fucked and I want you to slurp me. I spanked you last night, said Federico, recalling the melodrama of Bank Error in Your Favor. Well it wasn't sexy enough, she said. You weren't angry enough. Yes I was, mumbled Federico. She put a hand on her hip, then pulled the plug in the sink and the water spun down the hole counterclockwise as it always does in New York. I want you, she said very evenly, to force me to suck you while you're doing the dishes. But *you're* doing the dishes, said Federico.

She made a point of inviting a couple, friends of Federico's from *Variety*, for dinner, getting stoned, throwing them out when they had barely finished their dessert, then telling Federico she couldn't have waited much longer for them to leave because she wanted him to fuck her right here and now on the floor. He ended up using the twirly piano stool.

She began to mention another of her former friends, the infamous *Ignazio*, with whom, she said, she had always had a chaste but very deep relationship. You've just missed Ignazio, Ignazio dropped by this afternoon, Ignazio was asking after you and says let's get together for a drink when he's not too busy at *medical school*.

Y A W N.

Federico's girlfriend would demand him and then push him away. He thought, whenever I do or say something *fond*, she acts bored or gets pusillanimous, as though marriage and the future are to be reviled. She invokes Ignazio or smokes too much dope or makes me fuck Killer Barbie extra hard while she just gloats in the arm chair. His girlfriend was jerking him around the world, he thought. It was a circle jerk, if you could put it like that—or *he* was.

It was about this time that Tilly showed up. She was on secondment from *Variety* in London, where it seemed they had little to do. Well, what were they going to write about? Kenneth Branagh?

Federico immediately repositioned his desk and chair so that he could look up and see Tilly at any given moment. She had pretty legs and wore short skirts and provocative London shoes. She spent a lot of time typing what turned out to be a screenplay she was writing about Buenos Aires, where she'd grown up. Its maids and stray dogs.

On the third day that Tilly was in the office, Federico typed the following on a sheet of paper:

1. Hello.
2. How are you?
3. Dinner.

He took this out of his machine, stood up and took it over to Tilly's desk and put it in front of her. He pointed with a pencil to No. 1. She looked at it and up at him and then back. She took a pen and wrote *hello* next to his. Federico then pointed to No. 2. She nodded. Then he pointed at No. 3, which she read several times, and then wrote next to it in a pleasing light blue loopy hand, *Of course*.

This subterfuge was all because the section editor was a sick, snooping predatory bastard, who thought all the women in the office were his personal property, or were to be appropriated as such. Which Tilly had already surmised, as she told Federico by the elevator when they firmed up their plans.

Federico and Tilly really hit it off. They talked about everything. She brought with her some exciting bolshie London politics. Federico found himself wondering if he'd ever talked about anything with his girlfriend; the only exterior subject that came up these days was Ignazio. Tilly only had a few temporary places to stay, and within a week Federico had asked her to stay at his place, without thinking much ahead, it must be said. When he suggested this, she actually *turned a cartwheel*, right there in the Park at lunch.

So there were Tilly and Federico, down the street from Federico's girlfriend. He began 'handling' the situation by telling his girlfriend that he had several nights of heavy work, because of the *Golden Globes*, and he was going to stay alone in his place and TYPE, which she hated. He and Tilly stealthily traveled to *Variety* from different subway stops, in case anything should arise on the street. But this Cox-and-Box scenario couldn't last very long and he knew it.

One night Federico's girlfriend buzzed downstairs. He answered and told her to go away. You can't come in, he said, God damn it, the *globes*. Barbie's at my place, came the reply. Tilly, who knew the score, looked at him with her eyes which were as open and free as her handwriting.

Why don't you go down? she said. No, tell her, said Federico into the buzzer, for once to fuck herself.

There followed a week without contact. Federico nonetheless felt a happiness circling around, felt it to be desperately circular, like looking at Tilly's perfectly round spectacles, the end of the platen of her typewriter, the sun.

Tilly was so refreshing that Federico got drunk and wrote to his friend Rittenhouse, this friend he still liked and saw once a year at Christmas, even though he had turned out to have something to do with computers. Federico was always trying to convince Rittenhouse that he was missing out on everything by remaining in Minnesota. He always drank beer when he wrote to Rittenhouse and *lorded Manhattan over him.* Rittenhouse was impervious to this stuff because he had a car and a va-va-voom girlfriend who worked in fashion. She wore a tiny black leather skirt a *lot.*

Dear Rittenhouse,

Even though we are both twenty-five, I do not think you have lived. Because: you have never eaten carbonara at the Rocco Restaurant on Thompson Street until a late hour, and then walked hand in hand on a summer night all the way up Fifth Avenue to Central Park, hand in hand I mean with a girl, no, a WOMAN, a newly discovered delightful companion, who really thrills you in every possible way, with her smile and her ideas and her clothes. You have not found a late bar on 61st or 62nd

Street and then walked around the Park, not wanting darkness to end, and then when it does sitting down and talking, talking away at Columbus Circle and watching the city wake up, the businessmen and the tramps and the waiters, then getting something to eat in one of the timeless joints of Times Square, the pancakes from somewhere out there in America and the coffee out of an old movie, finally showing up in the office without sleep, but with everything else: literal lipstick on the collar, whiskers, a bottle of beer in your pocket and an erection nosing around in the pants of your suit.

Federico never got a reply because Rittenhouse had something to do with computers. (Rittenhouse himself had but a poor understanding of his job.)

There had been some stupid PICNIC arranged, months before, for God's sake. Federico was trying to be polite, he was trying to keep everything *going*, the poor man, so he went, gnashing his teeth all the way. He wanted to invite Tilly, not thinking through how *that* might be carried off (She's new in the office? Bah!). But she waved it away and he left her typing, typing merrily.

Being a Manhattan boy now, Federico had acquired the natives' distaste for transport, for *leaving*, really, even though if you never leave Manhattan you will eventually go insane and have to be institutionalized. He often thought that he resented the subway having wheels: he liked to think that it slipped along on a slick of some kind of oil, olive oil or *banana oil*, that would be it, and in a political sense close to the truth. He hated airplane wheels. They were so tiny. And train wheels, and above all the wheels of cars—they so often seemed unreliable and boastful, the wheels of this tarty and trashy-looking but very expensive car, the girl equivalent of a muscle car, this *tit car* in which Killer Barbie was driving them *out of town*, to the reservoir, what a fenced-off prosaic place for a picnic. There was nothing but water, in a cage, picnic tables, and an anemic wood full of trash.

Federico sat as far away as he could from his girlfriend and fumed over the measly meal and the cloudy day. She, to his surprise, was trying to make the best of things, handing out liverwurst sandwiches, stalks of celery and Kool-Aid, at which his jaw had dropped. She was no doubt replicating the picnics of her family, who were not exactly the most creative or sybaritic people on earth. How *had* they produced this beer-guzzling, cigarette-ravening, dope-fazed, mad-for-cock phenom.? Merely with their own distraction and proprieties? That all it takes?

And where had she got her predilection for castigation? He'd asked her once, in what had felt like a moment of intimacy, and she'd just shaken her head. So the only answer had been for Federico to take her over his knee—it was an unending, circular conundrum.

Nobody had to make conversation, because Killer Barbie had just been to our nation's capital. She blabbered a mile a minute about the Supreme Court building and its motto, inscribed over the portico, and how her grand-uncle felt about it, given what was happening in the government.

After the delicacies had vanished, Federico's girlfriend decided to pretend it was a sunny day. She was always doing that—she liked to think she could make things happy as she alleged they were in her childhood. I'm going to take a nap, she said, they're driving me nuts at work. She lay down on the bench.

Killer Barbie said, Let's try to find a place without all these cigarette butts, so I can smoke. She and Federico picked their way through the absurd wood. There was the occasional child's cry and the odd gun shot, but no one to be seen. She tiptoed her way fussily through the waste wood and its detritus. She might never have been out of doors before. Suddenly she fell over a big log she had been about to climb over, her sunglasses on the ground, her arms and legs splayed out like the spokes of a wheel. As long as I'm down here, she said.

The big log perfectly positioned her, rolling back and forth, giving them both intense sensations. As Killer Barbie began to howl, as the log gave her to him, and again, Federico felt as if he were on a ship; he looked out at the sheet of captive water and thought about the turbine, its enormous wheel, which must be out here somewhere, he thought, pushing all the water toward Manhattan, where he wished he was, lying on the floor next to Tilly, while she typed—he tried briefly to remember Thea's name. He really took it out on her, old Killer Barbie, whatever it was. Good old log!, with spirally, white-cut ends.

Jesus Christ, said Killer Barbie. Lookit the ass of my pants.

When they got back to the picnic table, Federico's girlfriend was annoyed. What's all this log rolling without my permission? she said.

It just happened, said Killer Barbie. She lit a cigarette that celebrated her satisfaction at having got Federico off on his own.

Everything was fine—was it not fine?—except it was just terrible. The fact of Tilly could not be explained and as time went on it couldn't even be introduced. What was more exasperating still was that Federico still slept at his girlfriend's several nights per week, the pretense of typing having worn out, and Tilly didn't even CARE. But Federico's girlfriend seemed to be starting to care, a lot, about almost everything, except him exactly. The more confused and noncommittal he became, the more full of plans she got—he felt at any given moment as if he were about to be talked into marriage and at the very same time made a cuckold, or a fool of. It seemed that his girlfriend wanted to board the train of matrimony and decency and all that crap, amazing considering her tendencies, but leave him at the station, his ticket in her hand—as if having taken Federico's name, the conductor or the engineer would do in practice.

One Saturday morning Federico kissed Tilly and went down the street to the other place. His girlfriend's mother was coming for lunch and it had been a while since he'd seen her. The mother was friendly and kind, and had even taken out a subscription to *Variety*. She was fascinated by the box office reports, while Federico didn't give a damn about them, which was disloyal to his employers.

The apartment was in an odd disorder, especially considering that a MOTHER was coming. There were cans and bottles around, roaches in the ashtray, and the place had a heavy fug about it of smoke, sweat, stupid *incense cones* and his girlfriend's perfume, Obnoxious by Revlon. She called Federico into the bedroom, where the window was open, and where she was standing amongst the blankets which she'd pulled off the bed. The sun was strong on the mattress, like a spotlight. And she started talking about Ignazio, Ignazio was here last night, we stayed up talking, Ignazio is my oldest friend, we really have a strong . . . He's very . . .

Everything is pointing at the bed, Federico thought—this *pantomime* of party clutter, the smells, the bright light. So, he looked at the bed. As she talked. There, dead center, was an (almost) laughable-looking *assembly* of strong, dark, thick, curly MALE pubical hairs. I'm not kidding, it might have been by Joseph Cornell. And there was a neat medium-sized wheel of stain, which Federico discounted as his own as he usually wore a rubber, either the bumpy kind or, when Killer Barbie was visiting, the one that makes you last longer. Did he feel calm, or amused, or angry about this? Federico couldn't decide. Maybe all these, but he didn't like to feel that way—he liked to feel *one* way about things. Most things. What was he supposed to say? Was he supposed to ask? He looked at the sperm wheel and then at his girlfriend, who was wearing a truly unreadable expression, and then went out to the kitchen to make a salad for her mother.

Lunch was fine, forcibly had the appearance of fine. Pasta, cheap white wine and news from the suburbs. The mother wanted to know why *Excalibur*, starring Helen Mirren, wasn't doing well in the Midwest, while taking more than respectable receipts in major coastal cities. Federico didn't know, except that it might have to do with the curious irresolution of Lancelot, whereas in most Arthurian literature . . .

So, goodbye, see you later. They went out to shop together as mother and daughter. Federico had been unable to evaluate his girlfriend or her face through the lunch—try as he might to send her, at appropriate moments, *burning rays of opprobrium* about the pyramid of hairs and the assertive swirl in the bed.

At one point he told himself that this must be another put-up job: his girlfriend had got Killer Barbie to collect hairs from her own lumpen boyfriend and drop them on the bed; they'd decided that semi-skimmed milk would do for seed. But this was ridiculous, he told himself. In the middle of practically demanding that we are now a permanent couple, that we ought to be planning our wedding, she fucks Ignazio, that ugly duplicitous turd, and rubs my face in it. Why? Does she think this will *focus* my concentration? Does she want me to rise up and challenge Ignazio to a duel? He'd love that, the swine.

Federico walked to Madison Avenue, where he often went to calm himself. There was a lot of rich-smelling luggage; there were shoes he'd love to buy for Tilly; the cooling tobaccos of the old world. He went through the revolving door of a fancy book shop—went around two or three times in it, an homage to Tilly who always did this. He found himself in art, examining a collection of erotic drawings. Usually he felt he hadn't much use for 'erotica'—best make your own—although Killer Barbie had a photocopied book of photographs of erections which she brought over sometimes (the original belonged to her grand-uncle). The three of them would page through it while getting high. Check out page thirty-seven, she was always saying. Federico meant to ask her if these were the penii of the Supreme Court, but he was always too high to remember and she didn't have a sense of humor anyway.

There was a guy, *Montorgueil*, in this Madison bookstore, some species of French maniac, who drew severe-looking women who toyed with young fellows, using lots of elaborate equipment—the overall effect was that of the Marquis de Sade having imprisoned Rube Goldberg. What were they supposed to be doing with these machines in their *houses?* There was a fine hard young man rotating on a wagon wheel—the boss lady was holding his cock, her hand in a delicate yellow leather glove, as his sperm shot like *flights of arrows* across the room.

Federico wondered what that would feel like, thought briefly of broaching it with Killer Barbie, then felt exposure, a parody, because he was examining this in a raincoat in a book shop, then remembered what it was like to be in bed with Tilly, talking with her, and what her mouth was like.

Federico telephoned to Sidney for advice, as usual. Hello, it's Federico. Wait, it's *who?* said Sidney. Rod, said Federico. Oh, said Sidney, you gave me quite a fright. What is it? Well, said Federico, she's laying all these *plans*, I think, and at the same time she pushes me away. I think Ignatz slept with her, she showed me goo and hairs in the bed. Who, said Sidney, *Tilly* slept with *Ignatz?* That *is* bad luck. Sorry man. No no, said Federico, Tilly's fine and I think I should fall in love with her. Hmmm, said Sidney. What about the, uhh—you know? The *occasional*. Oh, we're getting along okay, said Federico, we had a little picnic at the picnic. Well send her over here some time, said Sidney, oh my God what time is it, you know I have problems of my own . . . What problems? said Federico. I have two problems, said Sidney, the first is yesterday I discovered she's been taking her diaphragm to work with her every day, and I don't like that, I don't like it at all, and she wouldn't answer me when I asked her about it, she said nothing. Just glared at me and I'm paying the rent here for the love of God. Is this Marcie? said Federico. Secondly, said Sidney, it's the smothering. It was okay in the hotel, it was even fun, but now I feel she's smothering me at every hour. But I wanted to talk about *my* situation, said Federico. So you're telling me you've got two women who both want you, who continue to want, oh excuse me, THREE women who continue to, shouted Sidney, despite your irresolution? This is a problem? But, said Federico. I gotta jump, said Sidney. Why don't you rotate?

Federico had not a dream, but a *thing* he carried around with him, or about him, an elaborate fear, articulated and dramatized over many months, which was in constant orbit. He pictured it like the wheel-shaped space station on his fourth-grade lunch box—the space station they never built, with its own supposed internal gravity because of its slow rotation out there in the vacuum.

The thing was this: a huge, international, interplanetary meeting of women, convened in order to discuss HIM. 'The U.N. of You,' he called it. All the women he'd ever been involved with sat at an enormous circular table, covered in grey felt, lit from above by a glaring white light. There was a dramatic haze of cigarette smoke, perfume, strong coffee and Formosa oolong. The debate was free-wheeling and very frank, and included the past, and fantasies of the past; the present and its corollary imaginations; also the actual future and what *might* happen.

It was not always possible to stop this thing once it got going.

He was just too young, said his first girl, still dear to his heart.

I'll say, said the second.

But aren't you *eleven years older* than Federico? said someone.

Chairing the meeting, unfortunately, was Federico's girlfriend, and to her left was Killer Barbie, who had to have things translated into headphones, or maybe she was listening to debates in the Supreme Court. Or to the Eagles.

Federico's girlfriend would describe how he left her, and how he was *going* to leave her. I was only trying to get his attention, she said. It's so unfair—he *helped me move* and then I never saw him again. I called him and he wouldn't see me.

Good idea, thought Federico.

That's not how you go about these things, said that Vermont girl with the gingham and the apple cheeks.

You were fucking Ignazio, said someone, that sleazebag.

And how, said a girl no one knew, not even Federico.

I think this is all beside the point, said the Harvard girl. Let's talk about his cock.

No, said the bait shop girl.

Why not? said the Harvard girl.

Yeah, said Federico, why not?

Prolonged silence.

It gets floppy in graveyards, said one.

No it doesn't, said another.

Gee whizz, when the beer comes out, said the stripy T-shirt and bar stool girl from . . . ?

Yeah, said Thea. (*That* was her name!)

Now TILLY said, I don't know what you're all complaining about. The point is that he can't, or won't, live up to his convictions or his desires. Because he doesn't know what they *are*.

Excuse me, who are you again? said Federico's girlfriend.

Killer Barbie started snapping her fingers, but it wasn't to get the floor, it was *Hotel California*.

The guy needs a shrink, said someone.

The guy is a jackass, said another.

Here Tilly stood and spoke dramatically and movingly in his defense. But she was from London or Europe or something and was shouted down by all these so-called sophisticates of the eastern seaboard, thought Federico, tears in his eyes.

Many times it would seem as if things were going to come to a head, a vote of some kind. Debate would become heated about the value of Federico as a lover and guy, also his irritating habit of sharpening three pencils at a time, in bed, before going to sleep.

It's worse than crackers, said the Harvard girl.

But the vote, even when it seemed imminent, always dissolved in static.

In a merry-go-round of the ordinary type of the late nineteenth or early twentieth centuries, a central engine, originally steam-driven, now usually an electric motor, drives a series of flywheels and belts. The main wheel turns the platform of the carousel, the platform and canopy being suspended from a central pier, balanced on a ball joint. Another belt provides power to the punched music-roll and bellows of the *Marenghi*, the lovely organ and snare drum machine. If you want the horses and other animals to charge, or gallop, and you do, they will be mounted on brass poles, hinged at the floor and attached at the top by a U-shaped flange to a rod, which reaches back to a toothed track surrounding the central pier. When the brake is released and the merry-go-round is in motion, gears attached to the rods turn on the toothed path and cause the tigers and gryphons and ponies to move back and forth. In an even more exciting arrangement, they will be geared from above and below, allowance being made for a crank in the floor of the platform, so that your horsie moves up and down as well as back and forth. This is a useful example of the practical application of eccentric gearing.

As far as merry-go-rounds are mechanically concerned, the restriction of centrifugal force may also be mentioned.

Federico was in the Park on Saturday, waiting to meet Tilly by the merry-go-round. It was wet and there was no one near. Federico had begun to feel Manhattan spin, faster and faster. He had the seedling of a suspicion that this was because he'd not been grave enough about his career. Suddenly everyone was going to leave him behind! Sidney was going to become an executive producer, Federico's girlfriend would get a seat on the stock exchange, Killer Barbie on the Supreme Court. Federico would be left typing, next to his dusty window on 47th Street, telling himself none of it mattered because he was still only twenty-five, or twenty-six . . .

Standing in the drizzle, Federico thought: I'm no longer Federico, everything's falling apart—I'm Roderick again. I'm *Rod*, he thought, aghast, and he felt a little stiffy at being *Rod*, the name that frightened everyone, made them COWER. The best thing he could say for himself was that he was the axle rod of this wheel he could control no longer, but really, no—he was no longer at the center.

In his childhood Federico had fancied himself to have a scientific and technical understanding. Had he not wired a bulb to a battery through a knife switch? Could he not construct 'Mr Machine' without a blunder? He liked too the sound and the concept of 'centrifugal' and used it at quite a young age. But whereas he thought he understood the idea perfectly well (it was what was happening *now*— he was going to have to grab hold of something pretty tightly—Tilly's ankles?), whenever he *did* use the word his father broke in with: *No no no that's centripetal force you're talking about centripetal not centrifugal everybody gets that wrong.* Little Federico looked in the dictionary about this twenty times a *year*, and he still couldn't understand it—how could something spinning produce a force towards its center? It just didn't *feel* possible. Federico telephoned Sidney about it once. I think they're talking about a funnel, a water spout maybe, do you think? said Federico. You know, said Sidney, when you get into these three-dimensional things, I glaze over. I am literally glazed.

Tilly came walking along. She didn't look at many things, didn't look from side to side like Federico did, who'd lived here a *lot longer*, he thought—she wasn't acting like someone from *London*; curious.

She was wearing flat grey velvet shoes, dark green stockings and a neat suit, which went rather perfectly with her open countenance and intelligent eyes, black hair and red lips. She seemed to carry her politics, her whole open affect with her, effortlessly. Here is your girl, man, thought Federico, your real girl. It is as plain and graphic as day.

Tilly took his hand, as if *she* had lived here a lot longer, he thought. She started talking about *Variety*, something about the layout, how the headlines were set above a two-column article, should she suggest a perfectly sensible change to the editor?

He's a beast, said Federico.

They circled the merry-go-round, walked away from it for a few minutes, then were drawn back to it.

You seem sad, said Tilly. After I came here? After I came all the way.

From where? said Federico.

Is it her? said Tilly.

Federico felt distinctly like crying. He watched the merry-go-round with the frown of an unhappy child. One of a number of strange things on it was a fanciful-looking *bench*, big enough for two or three children, decorated with dolphins. This bench charged forward, and went up and down just like the horses and tigers. This galloping sofa struck Federico as being very like his girlfriend's bed, when he and she and Killer Barbie were in it.

Yes, said Federico, it's terrible. I love her and it's boring me *rigid*. And here you are. From where.

Hmmm, she said. She tightened her grip on his hand and they kept walking around. Is she someone who would have a go on this thing? asked Tilly.

The Marenghi started nervously to rattle its snare drum, not without style. Yes, said Federico, she probably would do that, in certain moods, although these moods are often fake. They pass quickly. But it's not *unlike* what she enjoys doing. Smokes dope and goes to the planetarium. Like that.

Why does she smoke so? said Tilly.

I don't know, said Federico. Maybe it's *me*.

What about the other one?

Oh, *she* doesn't smoke so much, said Federico. She's addicted to men is all.

Listen Federico, said Tilly, I don't know what to say. I love you and I'm perfectly happy with what we have. I type when you go down to her place and I'm always pleased to see you come back. More than pleased, you know.

Federico felt hot. He suddenly thought the merry-go-round was turning too fast for public safety. He was always ready to assign a hundred thousand volts of free-floating anxiety to some parent-inspired neurotic death-by-amusement-park-machine fantasy. The leaping dolphin sofa and the bold tigers were about to fly off the merry-go-round and injure people in the Park. Really hurt them.

SCREW

So let me get this straight, and I'm not trying to make the old joke, *let's get something straight between us*, as the lascivious priest said to the nun or the randy cowboy said to the cowgirl or the handsome SEC investigator said to Martha Stewart—but in fact that *is* what we're talking about, is it not? Your perennial but perhaps not very interesting *needs*, your fucking fucking needs? I'm tired of this, man, I really am, I love you like my own brother, but I mean I would prefer it if you could *act* a little more like my own brother. What's wrong with the way *he* lives? I mean what have you got against it? You don't see him running around all over the place, lying his head off to his *wife*, and *me,* and more importantly to *himself.* So you went through what, one marriage and one—what do you call it? Or that was marriage too? All right, two marriages, the first to Claire. The *singer.* All right, so everyone has an arty period. But *marriage?* What was so god damned pleasant about that depressing apartment by the railroad tracks, literally *by the railroad tracks*, I don't have to remind you. And how long had you known her? The only thing you had in there was that ugly little piano, and the sofa that smelled like the extinguished cigarettes of every Rockette that ever lived. A sofa like a *whore*. Do you remember the day I came over for coffee and I went into that cold kitchen with the red vinyl chairs and the circular fluorescent light, god those are horrible, and the only thing in your cupboard was half a can of Hills Brothers, a bottle of gin and an ashtray? What the hell were you people living on? And Claire was singing every night in that awful prime rib joint and her floral wrap was draped on the sofa and it seemed as though there was no life in the house at all, like you'd never be able to get the smell of cigarettes and small hours out of the place. And what were *you* doing then? The *candle shop*, oh yes, so as to be able to write the perfect songs for Claire, who is in the prime rib every night with all those middle managers and god knows who else, *postmen* probably. So she was the one doing all the work, sure it was hard work, granted, but you were both so depressed, almost immediately you got married, by the lack of songs forthcoming from your *desk at the candle shop*, and the railroad tracks and the ashtray. Everything just stank. Claire so beautiful and her looks going in this grey tiredness, and you, you were so depressed that you remained inert, unchanging, like some kind of *haunted icon of fear*, you never even seemed to need a haircut or a shave. But you weren't content to separate, oh no, well you did separate but no decision, no divorce, nothing doing! *You* had to move into the apartment opposite and *mull things over*, watch her come and go still on the same schedule, I remember you saying it was driving you crazy, you could even see her silhouette on the dirty venetian blind, removing and putting on the same smoky floral wrap, month after month, remove and put on, remove and put on, and always alone, she never came home with anyone and that depressed you too, not even a postman. So—any songs come out of that? *Smoky Dressing Gown? Half a Can of Coffee?* Who anymore is a song writer per se, aren't they all dead? You're always talking about Youmans and Harburg, aren't you, guys with a flair and a cigarette and a piano and a *market* and a *world*, that are all dead and buried? And what a community to try to posit yourself as this thing, at least you should've moved to New York, you and Claire, if you were going to try and make a living as some kind of *zombies*. So then, yes, that stuff with the IRS, and then Silicon Valley happened, lots of money, *gold in the sewers*, yes I remember, and *candles* were no longer the staple of the economy they once were . . . but what were you bitching about, you were never a hippie. I never saw *you* use a candle in my fucking life. Anyway—let's not talk about it. So then you decided that anyone who could write songs could write *ads*, so you got that job in that forlorn agency, what were they handling, local nurseries, shopping centers, those stupid restaurants out along Winchester Boulevard . . . this was a big improvement for you? A steady income in the creative field, that's what you said, I'm only, the opportunity to *write songs at your leisure*, although it didn't appear to me that you *had* any, between all the television and the beer and that empty gym blonde you kept saying was the *new Claire, I've found my new Claire* you kept saying, how could you be *that* blind? You see, that's what this place can do for you, even if you imagine you're some kind of free agent, a *degree*, well, my my, *step* right *up*, the whole place is geared to making you yearn for a house, a car, kids, dogs, cats . . . I don't know. The thing is, you can see everyone's doing this, it's the only way things are done around here—*normal*, and I use the term guardedly. It's practically *normopathic*, is what. But if you *kid* yourself about doing it, just because you're bored—the whole place is so fucking boring and I admit it—then things are going to get bad. So, then Vicki. And how long had you known *her* when you suddenly convinced yourself at the beach that because you were *on* a beach and there were what, waves? *birds?* and so on, and it was a weekday so all the office and computer people and postmen weren't there, so you could consider yourself some free arty type, that because she looked vulnerable and sweatered and cold, her hair blowing around like in a commercial, a much *grander* commercial than any *you'd* written, no no man, I've got your number on this—a *national commercial*, that this was the moment to propose? I mean, WHAT. You eventually admitted it was the birds and the beach and the wind and her hair and all that meshugaas, it wasn't much to do with HER. Very good-looking girl—grant you—yes her skin and her lips were, she looked quite fecund, but this is what I'm telling you, you're living in one of the biggest baby farms in the world and it's getting you, you're *unbalanced*.

See, suddenly being with someone you barely know becomes more important than yourself, your stated goals, not that I ever agreed with them. And you have to admit that living so near to your parents was not healthy—they kept wondering what you were going to do with your life, which meant when were you going to do something else, *go* somewhere else, they wondered it more than you did! You interpreted it as when are you going to get married and be just like us, which is not what they were saying but which everyone around here always *thinks* they're saying. People *believe* there is some kind of normality, they believe that *normative forces* exist, they *never ask* themselves why they should perpetuate the race or perpetuate the way they live, which they shouldn't, but it's not a force, it's merely their *belief* in a force. What, you don't know what I'm talking about? If they asked themselves that, they'd have to ask themselves a lot of other stuff and of course they don't want to do that, can't bear to go into any of *that*, so the killing, I mean it, just goes on and on. But Vicki, *she* didn't care about songs, or anything else, she simply liked television and money and apartments and cars and her brothers and soccer and avocados. No? How you thought you were going to fit into all that fucking garbage I'll never know. I mean, here you're always wanting to get married, *gotta get married*, I remember you saying it when we were only twenty-one, *I think I'll get married this year,* jesus who were you going to get married to? Bob Guccione? So there you go, you have this wedding, which wasn't you to begin with, this ceremony, in the *pines*? In *Carmel?* Pacific Grove, oh right, the cheapskate's Carmel.

And then you're suddenly Living Happily and you're sucked into all her bullshit, willingly I know, yes she was sweet and nice, the tedious conversations with *two* families now, not just one, television, the *soccer jugend* . . . Just Happy to Be Together and you should have seen your face. All the time it looked like someone had stepped in a puddle and then walked across your brow. Or dog shit, I should say dog shit. So this is going nowhere, we all know it, we don't know what to do for you except watch your puddle and dog-shit face burn all the time. What could I do? I had my own problems. The . . . thing. So it falls apart, of *course* it falls apart, you're the most screwed-up guy in the world, how is it not going to fall apart? The thing was, though, your *utter perplexity* at your *second marriage* not working out, when anybody could have told you. I'm not 'laying blame', I'm just saying. So then I go away to *Seattle*, seven years, christ what a, and when I come back, lo and behold, *lo and behold*, you're married to Bette and not writing songs, not having anything to do with your past, or your stated goals, but I find you are in fact *running the machine-shop at her father's company!* No, I'm just trying to under, who said anything about sell-out? Who? What the fuck would you have been selling out, precisely? I'm saying that you're in this place which is positively unreal, and you're grasping at straws. There's nothing around to grab onto, so you decide you'll go with the flow, which is fine except that you and I know there is nothing flowing around here except bullshit. That's how people die. They die of *acceptance*. Why should people *accept crap?* Accept, accept! The Buddhists are full of shit. They make me sick.

But here you are, no more songs, you're driving this *car* around, you got out of the south bay which more power to you, I wish I, and you seem to have become a mechanical engineer or a what, an industrialist of some sort, and I'm impressed, I really am. You chucked the songs, the nostalgia, the theatrical yearning for stuff in which *no one* was ever going to join you, who wants to live like *Dick Powell?* And you apparently learned just about everything there is to know about the operations of *Yerba Buena Screw and Bolt*, and let's not get into the implications of that name right now, but it does have implications you have to admit, otherwise why are we sitting here? So for the past five years you've been getting up in this nice home that Bette and, let's face it, her father have provided you, and I do like San Mateo, all that, it's good that you got out of the south bay like I said, man we're all crawling around down here like I don't know. Everything's so. But you get up at four thirty in the morning? And there is often a pleasing kind of fog which comes over the hills, through the pines and cypresses, from Pacifica and Atascadero; and in the early morning these pleasing fogs are wrapped around the old trees and the Spanish style houses from the 1930s in your neighborhood. The garage is silent and musty and you like that too, this is the best part of the day, I know, because this is what we're talking about: you're married and you're lonely as hell. Aren't you. You drive down the hill and the stop lights are still blinking yellow at this hour in the fog, sometimes you stop at the little bakery, the only place open at this hour—the girls make delicious soft French doughnuts and you keep the hot coffee next to you on the seat of the car. You drive through the freight yards and park your car outside Yerba Buena Screw and Bolt, the large sliding door of the machine-shop is ajar and inside Toole is there, turning on the lights and the lathes, he has coffee too and cigarettes. The big old machine-shop, which smells of rained-on wood, metal shavings, and heavy machine oil. And these smells you adore, in a way, because they are the smell of your new-found security, and even camaraderie—these aren't bad fellows at all, no, even though they talk about a lot of things you can only guess at. They could be hostile to you, your position, but they aren't. Not that *Toole* would ever have had a try at Bette, you . . . hope. There are other smells which help you to screw up your courage to be here, the smelly outdated photocopier, and the ham and cheese sandwiches on the catering truck which shows up at ten o'clock. It's a well-ordered place, the machine-shop, and yet because you became what you became you always feel a nervous dread here, because all these kind simple folk, who know almost by instinct more about screws than you do, are depending on you, you are their captain. Sometimes you feel like Captain Ahab. And you know that you will spend a certain amount of time amongst these pressures and smells *not* thinking about screws— your desk is not a lathe after all and doesn't require that kind of attention—but thinking about Bette, and the large sponge of disaffection which swelled and swelled and blocked your view of her. This is it, isn't it? You lose sight, lose the sight in your mind's eye, your *heart's* eye you might say, of your lover, your wife, it's obscured by the ever-growing sea sponge, the giant squid of our miseries, our traffic, our newspapers and our television and our kids. Some of this never makes sense, because although you join battle over the behavior and the appearance, the *future* of your child, you're both doing the right thing, as you see it, both fighting for the best thing to happen, and battle is sexy, is it not, and being on the same side, ultimately, ought to bring you together. And take television, why is it not a salve and a benefit to conjugal love, why when you were seventeen could you imagine anything better than to lie in your socks with your natural mate on a large sofa all evening? But now all you feel is that the fucking tube has put the screws on you, put the kibosh on you all evening—you both come away from it frightened for your income and your appearance and your nation— instead of cuddling and gentle stroking and connubial amusements, there has been furtive snacking and silence and the more the television puts this pressure on you to *be together* in its own particular way, with its own *gaze*, the emptier life seems and you wind up smoking and drinking like someone who was born in *Glasgow* for god's sake and at the end of every day here are only dirty dishes and re-sentment. And it was almost as if Bette went to bed in the tentacles of the giant squid of your problems, which weren't so unusual, were they? Except that *behind* all the everyday problems you had to face, you had the feeling that you were ebbing away. What happened to that unu-sually nice guy who made music, the modest one who was secretly so sexy, a suburban sex devil who could screw the living daylights out of his warm and pretty wife in the privacy of their Spanish bungalow and in knotting his tie the next morning give no hint of this kind of activity? Toole gets up to all kinds of lusty adventures in pizza bars, but for you we were talking the agreed desire of marriage, weren't we? Not *lust*. Let's use pure terms because we are talking about a fall, albeit a short one, or maybe just a series of short misfootings and troublings, from the various graces of marriage. And one's wife knows, *your* wife knew that you couldn't see her, she'd *become* the house and the car and the kid and the position you were in and her parents; she was like unto the front of an unfathomable computer, a giant computer out of a 1950s movie, blinking and beeping and doing something secret inside. When you're depressed your vision shuts down, it *perceptibly narrows*, and you find yourself perplexed as hell, for example, the dik she goes up and down in the usual manner, no?, but you can't see, can't envision the application of it to your wife because . . . well, because what? Because there was an argument about the school or the damn car or the god damn Thanksgiving dinner you have to drive all the way to Sacramento to eat? People have to do things, you *can't exist* without doing things. Unless you're in an iron lung or you're President of the United States. What's bugging you is that at some point you *willed your marriage to become an abstraction*, therefore to exist on the same plane as taxes and the subtler, non-human problems of the machine-shop. For men marriage is an abstraction, for women it is and must be concrete. For men *everything* is an abstraction and that's how we are able to kill and kill and kill. *Because* our marriages are abstractions. For a long time Bette never said anything, everyone has periods of fatigue, but eventually her usual expression of the evening was one of quiet, one of hurt, and the only answer you gave to this *rather large question* sitting there in the middle of your marriage was either more whiskey or more television. And it was more than a little enraging, was it not, *Mr Sensitive Soul*, to lie there on the sofa and realize you had the same big sponge or even squid in your house that thousands and thousands of others surrounding you did? The same problems, the *deadness* that they even unhelpfully melodramatized and mocked on the television right there before you? It ought to be one of the great and enduring pleasures of *existence*, not to put too fine a point on it, to fuck your wife. And for you and these thousands it becomes bloody impossible. WHY. Tension built and built and before long you weren't getting along with anybody, even Bette's father who had warmly welcomed you into the company since his own son Danny thought the screw business was only for mental cases and had gone crazy and married someone from the *eastern seaboard*. And things got so bad, you felt suddenly so lost in the fastener business (perhaps Danny was right), unable to see its functioning or its future because you'd abandoned your *wife's functioning*, that you all ended up consulting a high-handed SHRINK who treated only multigenerational family firms. *I've seen this all before*, that was *his* high-priced response to every problem that came up. Throughout the whole period of this family firm therapy, which cost the earth and which the accountant told you *was not deductible*, which made everyone in the family even more frightened and irritable about it, while *she*, the accountant, kept sending higher and higher bills, because *they were* deductible, you sat on the therapist's sofa and thought: Bette is going to bring up the lack of sex at any moment! And you thought, wished you had fucked; that morning at least. You thought ruefully that there was a problem with firmness in the family firm and that you were it. What you *had* done that morning was to paw weakly through *Vogue* and having satisfied yourself that women in sharp little suits still existed you drove to the office. That a solution? But everyone sensed your growing distraction and unease did they not? Your father-in-law, Toole, the man on the *catering truck* even. So you suddenly, at the age of, what, felt a restriction in your freedom, your *degrees of freedom* were diminishing. And being an honest fellow, except for that stint in advertising, you knew you had to have a conversation with Bette, Bette of the red hair and the pigtails and the sneakers and the ankle socks, you wished, you wished you could say to her sometimes. She was an honest sort of gal too so you knew it was coming anyway . . . And of course it was the raggedy kind of conversation that began during television and continued through surprise late-night drinks and dishwashing—Bette with her hands uncharacteristically on her hips and asking what was the matter with you, where had the sex gone, we used to make love all the time, and then with *some regularity*, what a horrible phrase *that* was, where *were* you sexually she wanted to know, these horrible *phrases* that were not accusations but which any man dreads to hear. *Dreads.* And how were you to answer? How did you answer? First half in anger and half in truth, that you were in fact *obsessed* with screwing (thinking wanly of the office, and not only that but Miss —) and in sorrow and confusion often found that you were thinking of nothing BUT screwing. All kinds of screwing. Who is it, she said, her hands fists now and her legs defiantly apart. Who do you screw? *Nobody*, you said, absolutely clearly so that you both in a wide-eyed moment realized there wasn't going to be that unnecessary *eddy of denial*, she did at least see that there was nothing to deny— that would have been beneath both of you, for you to have been skulking around like that, *thoughts* were bad enough but a *woman* . . . Nobody, she said. And at this grew softer, with the melancholy she had cloaked herself in and over which you had despaired for some months. Who do you *want* to screw? And, again, *Nobody*, you said, and although this was also true, in a certain sense, it wasn't going to work and seemed ludicrous. You both moved from the sink to the table; you decided to confess and speak honestly and thought of taking her hand but these things aren't done in America so. But speaking there *as* an American man in his kitchen, a man who went to college speaking to his wife who went to a better college and who was therefore more reasonable and who had red hair the glister of which was only slightly tarnished, you *decided*, didn't you, to be as honest as you could. And this was an error, to a degree, because you were trying to formulate honesty as you spoke it—it's not always a good idea to do your thinking out loud in front of your mate. But that was what you did, you tried to put into formula the totally vague and random sense of your lusts (desires). You told Bette your wife that you had made mistakes as a younger man, that you had always insisted that everything be LOVE, even the merest passing blowjob; nothing else was honorable or tolerable to you and you now realized that this had crippled you, there had never been a revolution for you and love and sex had never become separate estates for you and you were now a cripple and something had to be done about it. And you still loved her of *course*. Here Bette made rather a good point, you thought: WHY NOW? Why does it have to be on *my* watch that you fool around in the cockeyed dangerous laboratory of love, why not chill, man, you *better*. But no, you argued, I have to find the separation, the dividing line. Otherwise. Don't you see. So, then, to your astonishment: *OK, buster. You've got one month.* Jesuschrist and went to *bed* then, and even put her arms around you through the night like always. So here we are and the next day, being a businesslike sort of guy and not wanting to waste time, but also feeling curiously now nothing really but love from and for your wife Bette, you did what, you placed a *personal ad? Discreet afternoon encounters?* And isn't it spelled discrete? said the girl on the phone at the newspaper who sounded like she might even be the type. I don't think so, you said, discrete means separate. But you are, said the girl, arentcha? Separate? So it went in misspelled you found to your disappointment the next day and this may be, given the way things are around here, what a golden ass the whole place has become, why there was never a response from no females. This was your chance to get what you wanted *with authorization*, huh? You didn't think that this was a kind of *insult* to Bette?

You thought that since you had been authorized, you could get a certain kind of woman to free the dik from its shackles? That might have been a miscalculation. So anyway every morning for a week you scanned the mail for a response, you'd put all the mail about the screw business aside and hunt for something about screwing, which never came and never came. And this was a bad time to be doing this, as Yerba Buena Screw and Bolt had just been awarded a most important contract, *excellent news* your father-in-law told you one morning, pleased with himself and the firm but perplexed by the big pile of unopened screw mail on your desk and trying, you could see, to peer through what was obviously a thick rubber mask of preoccupation on your face; he was trying to see into you and it made you feel lousy. This was his 'excellent news': Yerba Buena Screw and Bolt had been selected to machine a new Worm Gear for the *cable cars*, said excitedly your father-in-law who'd always loved them, a glorious new Worm Gear for the motors of the California Street line, situated in the winding-house on Washington Street, and you were to be in charge of it and Toole was to make it! So now began many special preparations of the shop floor and you had to go in earlier than usual, but that was all right as you were getting nervous about any possible mail about screwing that might arrive and be tragically opened by Miss —. You and Toole paid a visit to the winding-house one day, he was in holiday mood and delighted in all the ornate machines and the smell of grease and the way the machines were *labeled*. Toole thought it most elegant to say No. 5 Wheel instead of Wheel No. 5. You noticed wedged against a wall a display of the lever mechanism used to grasp the moving cables and get *jerked all over town*, you thought. *Foot brake, wheel brake, slot brake and gong—you'd better keep them busy or you'll soon be going wrong!* You felt all screwed up and were inclined to confess to Toole in the place he took you for lunch after the official visit was over, some place he knew which served Hungarian goulash, which he amused himself by *constantly* calling 'Hungoulian garlash.' There was only 7-Up to drink but you attempted honesty, you told Toole that the great problem was to separate love and sex. I have never had a problem separating them, he said. You revealed your plan and situation to Toole and he said, not unkindly, *So, you're a worm that is not yet in gear.* This word *worm* stuck around a while, and smelled, and *occurred* to you when you were wrapped in Bette's arms which she still instinctively did. And every morning you observed the word *worm* on the paperwork and plans for the upcoming machining of the Worm Gear for the Municipal Railway, and felt a worm when you glanced at the pile of mail from which nothing about screwing emerged or would emerge. Your father-in-law was putting a lot of trust in you, placing you in sole charge of the tricky machining of this essential Worm Gear—and your wife Bette was watching, waiting to see what would happen to you and the dik in the time she allotted for your separation of powers, so you felt a heaviness, quite a lot of pressure from that side of the family. You'd sit at your desk, waiting for the sound of the catering truck, half your mind on the increasingly obscure problems of the Worm Gear, the other half on females, you'd screwed yourself up into an actual heat, because of the 'permission' Bette'd given you, or—perhaps—that you'd *imagined* she'd given you. No no no, fuck you, let me finish. In the top drawer of your desk was the business card of a woman you remembered meeting. And you knew you remembered her specifically because she looked quite like the first woman you ever slept with. Isn't that true? You'd had a pleasant conversation with this woman, some kind of *marketer*, and she'd given you her card and wanted you to call her about . . . something. So, you called her. Didn't you? WHY NOT *seeping* out of your poor little misdirected skin you called her from the phone on your desk, yes she'd like to meet, to discuss that . . . thing you were talking about. So not to beat around the bush, you met for the drink, had the sham or let's say unimportant conversation about . . . something, got the hotel room and took off your clothes. Outwardly, you thought, this is a very attractive woman—but she turned out to have this rather empty Bay Area personality; also she'd *honed*, that was *her* word, her body with the usual useless exercises to the point that you felt she'd created herself an exoskeleton, like an insect, that if you slipped while pumping away on her and cracked the exterior of her body, the interior would be found to be totally empty, inside insects it always looks like a deserted machine-shop—empty except for the little white blobs you'd just deposited there. But friendly enough to be sure, lovely enough—and there was also the view from the hotel room, which was as reviving as her tongue and/or the drinks in the mini bar. You drink *brown liquor?* she said in surprise. As often happens the two of you, who met up to perform this act which equally satisfied and perplexed, spoke of other bedly experiences, some of them disturbing, it always gets disturbing when you, I mean, doesn't it? So this was not what you were wanting, was it? Not such a simple screw. This exploration of someone you saw in a crowd somewhere, a meeting somewhere? It seemed utterly blank, in the end, because she had developed an exoskeleton, devoid of flesh, of sex. I have to confess I'm on a mission here, you said, to separate love and sex, it must be done. But they *are* separate, said the marketer, let me show you. But she only showed you the one. The sofa, the view of the city during that rather in the end vicious screwing, you thought in the car. At home Bette was in the background, out of focus in the kitchen, the coffee table with *Vogue* on it in the foreground; the dik still stirring led you there where you searched for sharp-suited, crunchy exoskeletonic women who looked like the marketer and you thought what *is* this, how is it possible to find a woman who is at most *a piece of paper* more desirable than your wife Bette there in the background, your wife who married you, who has beautiful *mammal's* organs, lips, eyes, who utters the most wonderful cries when you bring her to her pleasures, which you are very good at, yes your wife standing right there? Asking you how was your day? This Worm Gear is bugging me, you said, I have to do some research. Your father's depending on me and I don't know enough yet, Toole is becoming frustrated and impatient. Bette handed you your drink didn't she and tickled the back of your neck. Get into that den, she said with an unusually ironic smile, and design the biggest screw daddy's ever seen. You were going to be her Hiero. With your drink in your shuttered den you resumed your study of Archimedes, which in turn led to *Sir Robert S. Ball's Theory of Screws!*, we kid each other not, right? This is what you had assigned yourself to ponder, if the small displacements of a rigid body be subject to one constraint, *e.g.* if a point of the body be restricted to lie on a given surface, the mathematical expression of this fact leads to a homogeneous linear equation between the infinitesimals ξ, η, ζ, λ, μ, ν, say

$$A\xi + B\eta + C\zeta + F\lambda + G\mu + H\nu = 0.$$

The quantities ξ, η, ζ, λ, μ, ν are no longer independent, and the body has now only five degrees of freedom. At this you burst into tears! Weeping there in the den onto the big old book on mechanics, *crying out* about the restriction of your freedoms! This equation swam before your eyes as it had on previous evenings and you turned back to the pages on Archimedes, half thinking about screwing still, the marketer, her legs spread and her chill approach to life. Archimedes, in many ways like your father-in-law, was modest of his many achievements. He seemed really to know what was important in life and what was fucking not important—all his little inventions which helped so many, the Edison of the ancient world, he dismissed his inventions as being *beneath the dignity of pure science* and he never even wrote them down. Built a better mouse trap and snapped it on his own nose. Stabbed, run through by the sword of a Roman soldier at the capture of Syracuse, even though an order had gone out to *find Archimedes and protect him at all costs.* But his work on spirals . . . You turned back to Ball's theories and suddenly it was all there, staring you in your tear-stained face, thanks to Archimedes and Ball the knight the simple screw of the Worm Gear blazed out, hovered in front of you, the simplest screw of all, my God, you exclaimed, I've got it, this is it, eureka eureka. How goes it? said your father-in-law in the morning, *twinkling* at you in a nice way he had, seeing by your *face* that you had solved the big problem, the big problem *he* knew about, he knew nothing of your separation anxiety. You bounded up the stairs from the shop floor to your desk, to the plans the drawings so desirable which seemed to await you now like lovers, albeit of paper. A few adjustments, you thought, and the Worm Gear will be free—free to screw its way through the world and bring pleasure to tens of thousands. The Worm Gear would be freer than you, bub. *Adjustment,* you thought in the next second, that Episcopalian's disgusting phrase for how a man and a woman survive marriage, 'they made a good adjustment'—what an odor of buried babies and lamp-lit, tubercular sexual importunings. You thought of Bette your wife at home that morning, the way she'd reluctantly released you from her pretty arms as you raged to get out of the bed, charge forward to the shower, the office, problem-solving Man in all his ridiculous opera buffa, god. The plans fed into the machine, redrawn by the little microdeity and *Voilá* you said, handing them to a surprised and gratified Toole, who for weeks had been spinning his wheels, grinding his teeth and playing slapsy-bunny with an attractive pizza waiter across the street. Toole fed the plans into *his* machine, put on his visor and the men went to work. You stood there grinning like an idiot, suffused anew with the satisfactions of the machine-shop, its smells dusts and sounds and the impending baloney and swiss of the catering truck. And the machining of the Worm Gear was on this wise: while Toole and his soldiers applied the sharp spears of their CAD/CAM to the exquisite hunk of Japanese metal, you drowsed up at your desk, looking out your window at the intricate electric Yerba Buena Screw and Bolt sign—you mused uneasily on the *gap between* the screw and the bolt in this rich sparkly black and gold rotating device. Looking across the street, beyond the pizza restaurant and *its* exquisite hunks, according to Toole, you saw the potent sign of the Red Devil fireworks factory, that muscular red fellow running pell mell forward with his big fork, and your crest fell a little here and you thought again of the revolution, here you'd solved the screwing problem but not the screwing problem. Were you trying to turn yourself into *that* guy? *Why* were you trying to turn yourself into that guy? The laughable and familiar image of the adversary suddenly chilled you. Where had gone the fireworks of the marriage bed? A Simple Screwup You Can Make at Home. And now in deep daydream you approached Bette your wife, told her markedly your reservations, your desires, your regrets and from behind the little black number in which you always dream her she whipped out a placard upon which were painted a large grey well-machined screw and a baseball . . . *then*, you were screwing through the water in Bushnell's *Turtle*, blind as a bat and accomplishing nothing, but very slowly . . . then a story in which your father-in-law, Toole and the other men unscrewed all the bolts in the beams of the roof one night, so that upon entering the next morning the entire machine-shop would fall down on your head, crushing the life out of you hours before the catering truck would arrive . . . and then the slow rattles and squeaks you heard *from inside* as They screwed down the lid of your coffin. All this while downstairs they slowly and laboriously turned the Worm for you. Two days of this *meshuggeneh* drowsing and worrying. Bette sending hot meals. Then release, of sorts, a little celebration, the Worm Gear hoisted on chains and pulleys! Your father-in-law thanking Toole, thanking Archimedes here (that was *you*, by the way), the men smiling, little cups of 7-Up all around. Yaay! The shining pristine screw ceremoniously lowered into its special crate. At home that night you would have given anything to be inside Bette your wife—but by seven o'clock the triumph of the machine-shop seemed too small, and anyway Bette was still wonderful, but remote—waiting to see if your desire would ever be kindled by the proper fire. A grand though empty feeling the next morning as you, your father-in-law and Toole drove the Worm Gear up to the city, to its new home and final resting place, the winding-house, where it was joyfully received by those noble engineers, and gently gently lowered into its motor housing, newly decorated, No. 2 Worm Gear. When, with pomp, the great motors were powered up, it hesitated for the briefest moment and then slid into perfect life, all synergy,

the way a store-bought goldfish takes to its new bowl—
happily. Little cups of Schlitz all around, they know how
to celebrate in the winding-house. Your father-in-law
told you and Toole to take the afternoon off, handing you
each a bonus of five hundred dollars, very flat and fresh
from the autoteller, Have a blast, boys—and drove the
company truck off himself. So, a few beers, said Toole.
During these beers you tried to *explain*, again, you were
obsessed with screwing. I guess we all are, said Toole,
who was eyeing up this sailor, and suddenly disappeared
with him. Well? You took the California Street line down,
down, secretly the most delighted passenger clinging on
the outside, clangadaclang, the wind in your hair, knowing the worm was turning, turning for all. Screws can *lift*,
screws can *help*. And down near the bottom jumped off in
joy, didn't you, at the sight of a little prostitute all arrayed
in vinyl, a perfect little doll of a red yellow white and blue
Mondrian, how extraordinary and how sunny it is, you
thought. *Drop her at the bottom and catch her on the rise, easy
on the corner when the dust is in your eyes.* Was this perhaps to
be the—? There in the hotel room was her pussy, *framed*
by old Piet if he only knew it, as if in a shop window, the
little meal you made of her. Nothing seemed wrong, but
you were screwy as a squirrel. *Yes*: she had a *vagina* and
here it *was*. Rather more bottom but those *pants*, jeez. She:
What do the pants have to do with it? This girl, so geometric, so like the lovely mechanical plans splayed out on
your desk. The usual—the chair, the bed. Refreshed at
the mini bar, and the chair again. The next morning, lei-
surely talk over what was left of the 7-Up—you told her

of the need to separate, your mission, the clock ticking. *How* do you cast off arguments, teenagers, trauma, but also all associations, desires? I don't know what you're dithering about, she said. The way I see it, if you've got both, and you say you have, or did, then you're *stuck* with it. You don't dissociate it from the what, the screw business and the shouting and the teenager. Isn't it *dis-associate?* you said. Listen, if I were you I'd get going, she said. This advice *blazed out. Kissed* her, didn't you? Now for Bette your wife you purposely had yourself dazzled in one of those giant horrendous jewelry shops, selecting a slightly crude but interesting ring of silver and gold combined, braided together, you and she, the family firm and the Worm. Down, below Market Street for the train and the *home town*, though you never thought of it like that, welcomed you with its Spanish style houses and a few wisps of fog for your morning ruminations, your responsibilities. And you did what, you *burst in the door* and went running all over the house looking for your wife, and found her bent over a little awkwardly and endearingly, picking up the teenager's dirty clothes? And you moved toward her with the silver and gold ring, she straightened up, her face red not from bending but from outrage, hurt and abandonment, unknown to you she'd crossed the line, maybe it was yesterday. And she hit you so hard and so squarely that there could be no talk. Right? And then there could be no marriage and no home and no job, Archimedes, you were well and truly run through, which is why you have to talk to *me* about this. What do I think? I think you fucked yourself forever by trying to make something simple which is only everlastingly complicated. This was all so unnecessary, the wacked-out logic of the Horn. I think you've got more than a few degrees of freedom now and you should take it and go screw yourself. Frankly.

WEDGE

It is well known that strictly speaking the wedge is only an application of the inclined plane. But.

Here, at last, were people of quality: my girl had in her house a multi-level living room. From the upper level of the living room you could see to the rear of the house, and glimpse a small room which had a television and sofa in it—which is where I slept when her father was at home. My girl and I held a dubious theory that her mother once had watched us romp in this room, from the living room's scenic viewpoint. We felt bad about it because her mother was ill and this might have made her worse. But who knew? She might have been heartened by proof that her daughter was part of the human race.

My girl's family had had a most cruel wedge driven into it. Not to say a maul, not to say a *bomb*—her mother's schizophrenia. I attributed the quiet of my girl's house to this. When I stood by myself in the raised living room, or in the hallway, it often would seem as if something had just

occurred—a shock or an outrage of some kind, a crime—
and that the family, the house, had paused, afraid, and were
waiting to see what would happen next. The way people
hang around the scene of an 'incident' after the cops tell
them to go home. In the summer, with the silence-making
air conditioning, the house held its breath.

My girl, her sister, and their father all wore an expression of *scouting*. Their eyes were fixed in the middle distance, looking for wife and mother. Expecting her, hoping
to see her come over one of the green rises of their suburb.
I adored this look in my girl, even when I had ascertained
its cause. I liked it because I was sad and she was sad. I
liked it because it was thrilling when she took her green
eyes from the horizon and focused them on me.

My girl's father was the first girl's father I had encountered. He owned a successful business and wore soft baby
blue turtleneck shirts. When I dream of this family, which
I do still, he is in one of these shirts. He liked opera, particularly *Aida*, and he didn't like his wife being in a hospital. He often looked at me as if he couldn't see me—I was
something indistinct. I suppose he decided to tolerate me
for a while; he was nice enough that first year.

My girl's sister was still in high school. She had masses
of red hair. We held a dubious theory that she listened to
us making love from her bedroom on the nights I slept
with my girl. The sister was vivacious, seemed less trou-
bled about her mother than my girl was, attended to her
studies and wrote poetry.

In simulacrum of the mother was a cook. My girl's
father and mother had always referred to each other by

the nickname 'Cook', for some reason of honeymoon, and the use of the word *cook* caused vague disquiet, you could see that. The cook too seemed to be waiting and listening with the others, and often, I thought, wished herself invisible.

Our first summer together seemed a long one. My girl's father was away a good deal of the time and we more or less had the house to ourselves. We fucked a lot, read, and developed a pleasant diet of raisin bran with the addition of Tiger's Milk, which I believed aided our fucking. At night we had chef's salads. I felt masculine and free. My hair was long and I even used to wear overalls without a shirt.

Is there any more lovely fun than getting to know your lover's wardrobe? Through her clothes, so to speak, you are intimate with her and through her clothes you remember her. You become fond of her clothes by the same degrees you become fond of her. On the day we met, my girl had worn the perfect outfit for October: autumn-colored corduroy trousers, pseudo-hiking boots, a rust red cashmere sweater and a short houndstooth tweed jacket. Her auburn hair was clipped short and all this forest floor-iana made her green eyes very bright; unmissable. Wow, I thought, who has not seen thee oft amid thy store? Later I found this wasn't the kind of thing she usually wore— she was a child of the suburbs and most of her clothes reflected that: in fact she often wore things that were quite alarmingly glamorous, even out of touch with quotidian needs and, frankly, with her figure. On our first romantic walk together she wore a paratrooper black nylon thing with zippers on it—I'd never seen anything like it. But it was expensive. Hers was a family with walk-in closets and stacks of sweaters in different hues. She liked buying clothes and did it easily, not like me, who found a trip to Saks forbidding and grim. It's like mobilization for war.

I liked looking in her closet when she had it open, because I could learn her story there. She'd worn a purple suede skirt in high school. As with me, there had been a paisley period. Can you deny yours?

When she came to my place, during term time, my girl would lounge about in kid-like yellow pajamas, which nonetheless closely fit her curves. I would look out at the trees on the street and feel proud that this pretty woman with wet, dark red hair was using my shower, my soap, my pots and pans, and would soon be in bed with me. *Rather than just enjoying it*, my first love, I felt it destined, felt it needed and had to be.

I found it overwhelmingly wonderful that she loved and fucked me, and thought I had had the fantastic luck to land smack-dab in the middle of a wonderful example of the natural order of things: of course I loved her—we were fucking, weren't we? Like crazy?

She'd had other men, some of them much older, but that didn't trouble me—I left that kind of worldliness to her. Tra-la.

My girl had marvelous little feet—my love for which is *constantly mocked* by my so-called friend, to the point that I am considering no longer returning his calls. What does he have to be so high-handed about? He likes girls with toes so long, and noses so pointy, that they could aerate lawns. 'You like girls with little cat faces and stubby toes,' he always says in the changing room, when I have taken my clothes off. 'Why don't you send your girl to me?' I said irritably last week, 'I have some bills I need to spike.' But my so-called friend never feels vulnerable, even when he's naked.

My girl had marvelous little feet, and around the house that summer she wore a lime green cotton dress and a pair of cork-soled wedges with red leather uppers. The wedge is only an *application* of the inclined plane, but these red wedges gave her energy a specific bounce, made her calves look happy, and I liked the look of her clean, pampered little heels. She was a great *baigneuse* and exfoliatrix. One day when there really was no one in the house but ourselves, I took her on the living room floor—the red wedgies had induced an insistent ramp of my own. She was always very welcoming, and we fit each other well—yet another reason why I supposed we were already 'married', in the eyes of the gods.

I laid her down purposefully on the family's azure deep pile carpet, and the air conditioning kept things cool and quiet. The situation seemed to demand, or rather suggest, that I should be a little coarse. She was having a lot of fun, and perhaps going through both our minds were thoughts of her father, her sister, the cook, our dubious theory—her mother fortunately or unfortunately observing us that time. So we could have a rebellious thrill by fucking there on the floor, my girl in great voice. Who knows if we liked the thought of others being aware of how much we liked fucking, or if we were very private lovers letting off steam, being truly alone? I strove to give her pleasure, certainly more than once, which I was easily able to do thanks to Tiger's Milk and to the sight of her curvy legs and her little feet wedged passionately tight into the red shoes, which I studied for fun as I pushed again harder. I thought geometrically of the angle of the extreme stress of our union and related it to the angle of her feet in the red wedges. I went on, it really was marvelous on that carpet in the silent house.

'Take off my dress,' she said—which she perhaps desired because of the 'wantonness' of the situation. But I said No. She asked again, in a higher voice. Again I refused. But I wasn't saying No out of sadism, or playing the role of a *masked burglar*, there on the carpet, although I would have if she wanted me to. I said No because I loved her green dress. My girl in her green dress and red wedges was summer, and I was making love to my girl and our wonderful summer at one and the same time. After that day the simple appearance of either her green dress or the red wedges was enough to make me ready, immensely ready. And when I dream of my girl, which I do still, this is how she is dressed.

She was a year ahead of me at college, and while we were both there, that was fine. We took an interest in each other's books. I studied at my place while she preferred the library; once I came across her there and she blushed. 'Now you've seen where I work,' she said. I'd come between her and something private. Even though there are other people around, you can always proclaim a nice wee kingdom for yourself in a library. I thought that this library kingdom of hers might have to do with some of her previous men. Had they been allowed to meet her there? I affected not to care. She had chosen me, and that was of course *pre-ordained* and very necessarily right.

With her green eyes my girl read O'Neill, Wharton, Bancroft, Faulkner, de Voto, Emma Goldman; lots of history and literary and social criticism. It was American Studies, at which *We* in *The Department of English Literature* quietly scoffed, with our shiny new *pipes*, though I admired her dedication and the breadth of her interests. Her senior thesis was on Alfred Kazin, and it was very good, though I didn't care about Alfred Kazin; her major professor thought it was excellent too and she didn't care either.

In April I told her to send it to Kazin, he's still around, why not? Guy like that might be flattered to read something *sensible* about himself. She looked at me in a doubtful, then encouraged way which made me melt. She hemmed and hawed, but finally wrote him a graceful note, and dropped her paper in the mail to him, at what I imagined to be a book-crammed, filthy apartment on Union Square, the great socialist riviera. I remember the weather of that month very clearly: the days were dry and bright and the trees in the park waved new green leaves at the bluest sky. My girl would be graduating, but I never thought that would be a problem. Meant for each other.

Weeks later we were studying together in my room one night and she looked up from Djuna Barnes and burst into tears. It might have been a lot of things—it might well have been *me*, but she said she was so disappointed she hadn't heard from Kazin. Here she'd sent her senior thesis, on Kazin, a thing she sincerely believed in and had crafted with dedication and even love, *to Alfred Kazin* and he hadn't bothered even to write a coffee and urine stained postcard. My heart broke. I said I would take care of it.

The next morning I typed a burning letter to Kazin. I upbraided him for ignoring an excellent piece of work sent to him in all sincerity by a promising student with a bright future, with green eyes, called him several clever names, and no kind of scholar, and actually, in the end, challenged him to a fist fight: *I call you out, Kazin. You ignored a brilliant girl at your peril, you dissembling Commie geezer. Union Square, man—Thursday. Four o'clock.* The letter was pages and pages long; I was fantastically steamed. I wedged it into an envelope and ran with it to the post office. He never showed.

She graduated, wearing a pretty summer dress from Henri Bendel under her robe. She was keen to find employment—otherwise she would have had to work for her father, who, though successful, had a very depressing, noisy office. She quickly found a job in the library of one of the historical societies, which suited her perfectly, because of her academic bent and achievements, and because the society was just off Madison Avenue, close to her favorite stores.

So began our second summer. I was insisting to myself that everything was as it had been—she stayed with me most nights and went off to work in her yellow Volkswagen every morning. I was happy, but unaware of how quickly the grotty charms of university pall once viewed from outside.

My girl's father, I guessed slowly, had been assuming that I would evaporate when she graduated—that I'd disappear from his horizon like the tuition he'd been paying. We often went out to the quiet air-conditioned house on weekends, and as time went on he was less and less pleased to see me. I couldn't entirely account for this, because I really am a great guy, but I got the niggling idea that it had to do with religion. They didn't really practice, but of course that wasn't the point—people like this think you can't *know*, won't ever *understand* . . . I think he was starting to tell her such things about me. 'What about when he turns around and calls you a dirty so-and-so?' Ahh—I saw him on Sixth Avenue a few years ago and felt in my heart I still liked him fine, even though he avoided me. But my place in the family had changed; I was sitting less comfortably in it. I was something undesirable. I had been wedged in.

But I was not without doubts myself. My girl had always seen a shrink, so what. Well I say 'so what' now, big man, but then I was hostile to all that kind of thing. Youth scorns the idea of irresolvable problems. It seemed a big basket of secrets she kept from me, which I didn't think suited her, and I felt it a wedge between us. I got angrier and angrier about it, which was *displacement* (excuse me) really, because I *should* have been getting mad at her father, at his unfairness, his refusal to know me. I was angrier at her *shrink* than I had been at *Kazin*.

One day we were in her suburb, in her yellow Volkswagen. I still remember the license plate: MTW 145, mostly because after we split up I continued to see her yellow Volkswagen around the neighborhood, around town—for a while I seemed to encounter it everywhere, which would make me fly into suspicious rages . . . Then I began to see nothing *but* yellow Volkswagens, they had all been ordered to drive past my building constantly . . .

On this day she left me to wander around the commercial district of her suburb while she went to see her shrink, who had his office in a two-storey dull red brick American 'professional building', as the strange saying has it. I imagined it to be tawdry, I conceived the whole enterprise to be *tawdry* and as I walked around looking at a profusion of sweaters in different hues and overpriced pesto I fumed and fumed. This was sort of dangerous—she'd never brought me physically this close to her analysis, and her analyst—she would always leave a cushion of several hours after an appointment before agreeing to see me, and that drove me nuts as well.

I met her at the car at the appointed time, and she looked vague, even injured. Her green eyes were firmly fixed in the middle distance. But did I have a cruel desire to see her at her most vulnerable? I think, with regret, that

I did. I was out for blood . . . She said she wanted to buy some pesto, or a red sweater. We got in the car and drove up the boulevard of the commercial district. I couldn't stand her uncomfortable silence any longer, and I flatly demanded, like an idiot, like the stupid and callow Philistine that I was, what the hell exactly goes on in there with Doctor Sloss, his very name nauseated me. She looked frightened, and very sorry that I was in her car. But she told me, quietly, some of the things they were working on, psychoanalytic truths for which I was just too young. The simple adversarial *facts* of our brains and our genitals, that fearful people so love to mock, when you can see *them* floundering around in this very stew of their own fucking problems and ignorance: 'He says I've really always *wanted* my father.' This so startled me that I blew my stack. At this point we were coming back along the boulevard and passing Sloss's professional building, the pesto sweater place having been closed for lunch. I rolled down the window and shouted, 'Fuck you, Sloss!' right as we passed. I was hyperventilating. My girl's green eyes filled with horror, and with such pain that I hoped we would immediately have an accident and that I would be instantly bloodily killed, while she would be thrown clear. But I managed to *retain my anger*, if you can credit it. 'I can't believe you did that,' was all she said. And I cannot remember where we went or what we did that day; it is completely gone.

She never made reference to this brutish occurrence.

After a while, in my callowness, I assumed she had forgiven me. But now things began to change. Things started to wedge themselves between us, such as the idea of the *real world*, I thought, *invading* the last year of my studies. The idea that things might shift, move on; the thought I might lose her.

She was still coming to see me and I still went out to her suburb, but I had lost my foothold there, if as I say I had ever had one. Our fucking acquired odd, desperate qualities. One night we were sitting at the kitchen table in her father's house—the formerly gay table of chef's salads and Tiger's Milk—having an argument. She was finding me younger and stupider all the time; probably it was about what I was to do when I finished college. I see now that I was in no position to offer her *anything*, as she could see that I was going to be one of those people who live like students, with *student* aspirations and *student* opinions, for years after they graduate. So what's college for, anyway? While I listened to her, I put my foot in her lap. It crept slowly toward her pussy while she was talking. I started to tickle her with my toe. She looked surprised but continued speaking. She smiled and slid two inches down in her chair. Finally I wedged my foot firmly under her and vigorously made her come with my big toe. As she came the argument seemed to conclude, naturally, grammatically, and—musically. We looked at each other in some amazement: there was something not-us about this moment. We could see it.

Things slid, but somehow we carried on, went on. I was losing, I was going to *lose*. I tried to grab things. I insisted that she take us to the family's white weekend house in New Hampshire. I insisted that we make love roughly there, with extra Tiger's Milk. I insisted that she teach me to *drive*, what a thing to demand in that emotional climate. And on those roads. I was hysterical and couldn't get the hang of the yellow car that I loved. I had completely terrified and exhausted her, and on the way home, after to my own surprise I had brought up the subject of marriage, which really hadn't ever been mentioned before, my girl's green eyes filled with tears. 'I can't marry you,' was what she said. She said something haphazard about different *concerns*, *backgrounds*, and I knew her father had finally got through to her.

The rope was running out of the boat fast. On several occasions I tried to console myself with wine, with my fellow students, but this didn't work at all and led to a scene most unhelpful to my cause, when she picked me up in a dreadful state at the bridge and took me home and *nursed* me, while her father ranted outside her bedroom.

One day my girl told me, rather *casually* I thought, that she'd been to the apartment of one of her co-workers, a professional history nebbish whose pride and joy was a large HO train set. He'd put on his blue and white engineer's cap (I supposed), showed her how the layout worked, this is the night freight, this is the 5.10 for Mt Kisco, and then had taken, from his stripy engineer's overalls, his prick. With a red bandanna tied on the end of it (I supposed). At which point she'd 'left'.

I started in my advancing loneliness and fear to have fantasies about my girl's sister—I was sliding back into something odious, because before I found my girl I had had *only* fantasy in my life. Late bloomer. My girl had told me that they had discussed our sex, that her sister was curious. She'd even told her sister about the day she'd kissed me and then measured me, which made me embarrassed but secretly proud. I imagined that after listening to us one morning, my girl then gone out, to her shrink, or for pesto and sweaters, her sister would come and offer herself to me. This made me feel terrible, to force that kind of a wedge into my thinking about my girl, thoughts like this were a kind of log splitter of the emotions. I imagined my girl's sister *bouncing*, her red hair in pink ribbons flying about, and in doing so wasn't I just thinking that I had to stay here, *somehow*? Wasn't the ridiculous, prideful fantasy that I could stay in the family, eventually abandoning my girl, having realized that her sister was my true love, and everyone accepting that, even their father, and that things could, mercifully, *still be the same*?

In the face of disintegration we continued to screw; we were young. Why shouldn't you carry on with that, even if everything else is going to pot? And as I said, it was getting 'animal', though that is a tricky word. My girl had wonderful breasts and early on we discovered that we both enjoyed me to make love to them. I loved the feeling of heaviness in my cock when it was in that delicious groove; she'd dart her tongue out to the head when I thrust forward. This we felt to be very intimate lovemaking and my girl would wedge the door shut with a big wooden doorstop handcrafted in New Hampshire. The nicest thing about this was not the pleasure of *symbolism* or perversity or breast-madness, but that I could *feel her heartbeat* when I fucked her there. And she said she could feel mine, too, pulsing in my cock.

Despite our impending divergence, which was emerging as a recognizable pain behind all our dealings with each other, I was kneeling astride my girl one day, and we were doing this, when I suddenly had a kind of awful epiphany. And despite what a lot of people and even *saints* say, I don't think you always want to be having epiphanies; they can really get in the way. And who knows if epiphanies are accurate or true? But I was looking down into my girl's green eyes, at her red mouth which was saying sweet things to me, as she always said, and then I looked down at my cock moving between her breasts, and suddenly I stopped, at a forward point, and looked at it there. It seemed to look back at me as if awaiting instructions. As I stared at it, my girl's expression changed from one of passion to disquiet—she withdrew her tongue between her lips. I stared down at my cock, wedged between my girl's breasts, and thought god damn it o no o no, this is *me*—I felt a huge, nauseating wave of shame and guilt, for I was looking down at myself (of course) but suddenly my girl's breasts seemed to be her *and her sister*— I admit to indulging in my fantasies of her sister during our lovemaking, as things got grimmer. Yes, some times when I came inside my girl I was thinking of her sister, her red hair and ribbons bouncing. If you've never done this, never thought this, you must be crazy. I moved my cock up and down, yes, there it was, plain as day: I had forced myself between them. And then the feeling became starker and more unsettling, as I continued to look at my immobile cock, as I realized that it really was me, the very picture of stupid, priapic me and how I had wedged myself so uncomfortably and unhealthily into this family. And the whole thing *did* start to look unnatural, and wrong. I realized there was a struggle for power here. I hadn't looked it in the face until I'd looked at my cock, which was so still now it seemed like an unconvincing log in a bungled pastoral painting.

A wedge is *driven* by something. Mine, I thought, this wedge that gave my girl pleasure, and that has also possibly invaded the consciousness, or the daydreams, of her sister, was driven by longing, by love, by the very problematic hormones of possessiveness. And what drove her father's wedge, that was now pushing me out of the family, was fatherly love and the desire to protect, certainly, but matched, and I am sure exceeded, by bigotry, fear, and jealousy. And we know how strong those things are. Don't we, boys.

My girl was looking at me quizzically, holding her breath, and with a smile I moved gently down to my more usual station. I embraced her fiercely, and she began to move with me—although a strange and frightening thing happened. Instead of gazing at me in affection, as she usually did, her eyes once again regained that middle distance, that place where I did not exist. This filled me with fear, but also with ardor. When you're young you put all that fight-or-flight stuff into your cock. We began fucking harder than we ever had before—harder than I might have believed either of us to be capable. I was no Tarzan or jock, and my girl was used to an easy life—while passionate and giving, she wasn't someone who struck you as a primarily sexual person, though I might be wrong there. We fucked like demons, Martians, cowboys and Indians— I remember whispering that I felt I was going to burst out the other side of her—and the thought came to me that this was the last time we were going to make love, the last, and I didn't want that, didn't want that at all. But it was, *was*. I started to heave uncontrollably with sadness as we fucked so wild, and the convulsions of my grief translated into the thrusts of the machine of my body, which brought my green-eyed girl to her, our, last orgasm.

Shortly after that night, when we had been torn apart in our most intimate union, my girl told me that we weren't to see each other any more. The *different concerns*, by which she meant that she could no longer see her way to be involved with someone of my religion, although I didn't have one. I found the whole thing unbelievable, shattering—I'd foolishly spent so much time and intellectual energy on my belief in our inevitability, that to have this ordinariness, this *real world crap* dolloped onto my plate seemed perfectly impossible. I found I could believe in nothing, couldn't take anything in or make sense of it, and retreated to my apartment, stopped reading or working, and just sat, looking at the holes in the grey plaster. After a week I managed a journey to the delicatessen, broke out sobbing and ran out without my sandwich or cigar.

I awoke one morning with a heavy, oppressed feeling. This huge problem had been driven between me and reality. I put on very few clothes, my shoes without socks, fled my apartment and my street and ran, pell-mell, all the way up to the bridge. The eastern end of the bridge was firmly wedged in gneiss and schist, in our life in the city; the western end of it in trees and parkways, the life she was choosing to retreat into, the green suburb and her father's paranoid manipulations and prejudice. It still amazes me to think that I ran all that way, over the bridge and through interchanges and suburban roads that I only partly recognized, never having come here on foot before, but always in her pleasing company in the yellow Volkswagen.

Finally I was on their street, which had one of those names made up of two bucolic syllables, but which I had nonetheless admired because it was the name of *her* street. I ran up the drive and banged on the front door of the house, which was cloaked in its usual aura of electronic silences. It was about eight in the morning. My girl opened the door, showed not much surprise, and behind her was her father—they had both been preparing to leave the house. They were very cool to me—I suppose they weren't exactly surprised that I might do something like this, a *callow hysteric*. Her father went off to work, having nodded the merest hello, casting looks at my girl: you deal with this. In their coolness, of course, I got my answer—a *bridge stunt* was not going to bring anything back. But what I have carried with me from that first sight of the two of them, in their cool hallway, is the belief that whatever my girl thought and whatever her father thought and whatever *Doctor Sloss* thought, they were paired together, he and she, in a various search for wife and mother. In a way, it was a marriage—and I damned the idea of its consummation.

My girl kindly drove me back to the city and left me at my door with low, encouraging, distinctly distancing words, and drove off, MTW 145. Over the coming months I saw her car everywhere, all over town, a bright yellow wedge between me and my neighborhood, the rest of my studies and the rest of my life. If I happened to see her when she was driving, if she happened to see me, my girl would blink and smile and wave bravely. As if *she* were the one in pain.

PULLEY

Got to raise something heavy here. Having excluded myself from the world of women by my damned bungling,
hoist by the petard of my own stupidity, my youth and
inexperience, I floundered about in loneliness, New York,
and ill-conceived longing. What was worse, this all took
place on Amsterdam Avenue. I was in a perpetual fret
about what women were like on the East Side, but I had
no way of meeting any and I still haven't.

I used to think that music went with things, instead of
existing on its own, being in fact gloriously isolated from
us and all our bullshit. It was autumn and I found myself
forcing a connection between the light in the trees by the
cathedral—I've always been fond of those trees, although
the cathedral is hideous—between the light in the trees
and certain quartets by Haydn. It was the same kind of
thinking which had once enabled me to convince myself

that I was learning the French language, when what I was doing was sitting in the Maison Française with a little book on Utrillo in my lap, and scrutinizing the trees on West 111th Street as if they were in Montmartre. I failed French, they failed me for this.

You can't shake off European ideas around this neighborhood. You can drink in any decade you choose, Monsieur, with the cigar smokers of 1910, the coke snorters of 1990 . . . My mania for combining and confusing things was never healthier than it was at this time. Even now I can barely dis-associate those quartets from the leaves and the light I'm talking about and the cake shop across from the cathedral, which in those days was part of my syndrome of Parisian pipe-dreaming—everybody suffered from it in one way or another. And I can barely separate the cake shop from Nina, the only person I looked forward to seeing there. All the rest played chess and looked like big disappointments to their families. The worst looked like graduate students. What a life! Who wants to shave with the same blade ten times?

The cake shop was dim, it was never illuminated by the fluorescent sconces on the walls, which were bathroom fixtures of the 1950s. The interior of the cake shop was as dark as the interior of Nina. I don't mean I'd ventured to her interior yet, I mean her soul was dark, possibly purposefully as dark as the inside of the cake shop, dark as coffee, dark as gnostics would permit, whoever they were. She had gnosticism and pots of coffee and two neurotic parents she had to insult or even bury alive. She was very hungry for stimulus. She almost never slept, on purpose, so that everything would overwhelm her.

Nina looked as though she'd never been in the outside world—by the time I got to the cake shop, whatever hour our appointment, she'd have been there a long time already, smoking like she'd stayed there through the previous night. Or sometimes she would appear suddenly at the table, when I was sure the door hadn't opened . . . not to say she was other-worldly, just a neurasthenic girl from Brooklyn.

Charles Dickens wrote about how attractive he found women consumptives—the paleness, the manic shimmer to the eyes, the fluttering breath. Probably really dug them *breathing their last*, how adorable. He'd have loved Nina on sight. She was as white as a sheet if you saw her in direct sunlight, but I almost never did. She had thick black hair and large black eyes, arched brows and a very wry mouth. She affected tight black clothing, what are you, some kind of beatnik I used to think, when I was frustrated and annoyed—and watta bilt, I mean real classy zaftig from Brooklyn Heights! She batted her eyelashes constantly, a little less when she had a cigarette in her hand. Caporal seemed to match her ideas of what thought was, too.

She suited me exactly. I was still messed up with these French *problèmes*. When I'd go to meet Nina I sometimes wore a beret . . . it wasn't the only beret in New York, I grant you, but still. Amsterdam Avenue? I'd bring my pipe . . . fortunately I am wall-eyed, at least when I'm nervous or tired, so I'd drink coffee and think I was Sartre, no—I felt this explained Sartre, that it reified what he'd written in me. Can you believe this? To have a mystical belief in

Sartre—he would have knocked me to the floor. And spit in my eye, the good one. But other times I took a raincoat and a bigger pipe and drank little beers and felt like Maigret. Well, is there really a difference between Sartre and Simenon? If you're disaffected and suffering the horn and trying to cast a cold eye on life, on death?

I was frightened of Nina's intellect, to be truthful, but I found her so attractive that I was prepared to endure anything, say anything, read anything in order to keep up with her. Our encounters, our 'situations' were strange because I couldn't really explain much about the stuff which I seemed to find so important—she didn't go for fiction much, as I found when I tried to tell her about *Nausea*, Roquentin imagining a piece of meat crawling along in the gutter. That seemed much clearer to me than the two chapters of *Being and Nothingness* I'd managed to gag down. In my beret. There was something a little cruel about Nina, I'd reflect in the evenings. She insisted I talk myself blue in the face about existentialism, but when I asked her about gnosticism, or the gnosts, she retreated behind a feline veil of knowingness and massive eyelash action, as if she were a freemason, as if she was struggling in an obscure, ancient ceremony, with torches and books and knives, to know things of intolerable depth. Well, what do they actually got? I said. She had a petulant, spoilt suburban throb in her voice when she got worked up about something, which made my cock throb too, there in the rear of the cake shop.

She wouldn't go anywhere but the cake shop, wouldn't go on a date—I supposed that in going anywhere but her apartment or the library or the cake shop she thought she was straying from gnosticism. I had Sartre so I was mobile; I got around, savvy, soaked up atmospheres, like Maigret.

I simply cannot remember how I managed to find myself lying with her on her surprisingly agnostic black leather couch, which barely fit in her little front room. Her place was totally ascetic, bare linoleum, one white mug and one spoon—and only the couch—the bedroom was full of stacks of books. There were several hours of frottage—the jeans-to-jeans friction of those days. It turned out Nina couldn't imagine sex, couldn't quite picture it, at least with me, even though she'd told me often enough, infuriatingly, in the cake shop that she'd had it, a lot of it, somewhere in her pre-intellectual past.

Heavy petting they used to call this, in the sex warning films at school.

Her black hair against the black leather of the couch; her happening figure in her happening clothes. This doesn't seem very existential, she said. What do you mean? said I, what could be more? She took no interest in my cock, no interest in seeking it out. She only looked at me *adjusting* it, not *it*. I was starting to get a strange Sartre feeling— she was somewhere in there, hiding in her body, wearing it as well as her clothes, like a costume. Or maybe this was more a Maigret insight. I presented. Well—if you wanna, she said. That's the spirit, I said. Her black turtleneck sweater—she was far away inside it, many gnostic levels down, or up. It was the only Nina in the room. So I fucked it, like a cat would.

We kept meeting at the cake shop, but nothing was ever said about my cock. She didn't invite me to her place again and she'd flutter her eyelashes or stare out at the street if I gave her one of my patented direct existential looks. Once in a while she gave *me* a direct look, when she was buttoning her coat, but it never led to anything. Then there was a period of a few weeks when she started putting her cheek up for a kiss, when we met or we parted, but that ended. We began to meet less frequently; I still found her alluring, fascinating, but I had to admit that I'd failed to explain Sartre to her satisfaction, and I wasn't getting anything out of gnosticism, whatever it was.

I ran into her girlfriend and we went to the cake shop. So how is this caper with Nina going? she said. I can't figure it out, I said, we slept together once and then Pffft! Slept in your clothes, right? she said. I gave her the look. How are you anyway? I said. Pretty good, she said. I had a showdown with this guy I've been seeing. I was trying to clear the air, but he doesn't listen, because he thinks he has to be dominant—just because he's the one who puts on the, I mean you still have to listen, right? Outside the . . . *situations*. Probably, I said. What's your thing about Nina anyway, she said, if it's not intellectual and it's not sexual? I think it maybe has something to do with coloration, I said, her hair and her skin and her lips and the sofa. This guy wants me in fire-engine red lipstick all the time, she said.

I hadn't seen Nina for several months when she telephoned with that bleat in her voice, so we met at the cake shop. She looked more polished, glossier than before—sometimes she had a powdery, brittle look, as if coffee and cigarettes were desiccating her. She put her cheek up for the first time in a long while. I had brought my Sartre pipe but wished it had been the Maigret. Her eyes and hair were quite stirring . . . I felt something . . . I plunged. Let's talk about gnosticism! I said. She gave me a narrow look and started talking about her girlfriend, how the boyfriend wouldn't, couldn't stop being dominant, he takes her to the moon, but later he shouts about their goldfish tank and income tax. Maybe she needs to change her lipstick, I said, so to speak.

Well, she said. I am now doing *private* research on gnosticism. Jesus, I said, how could it have been more private than it was? Again with the narrow look, and then she told me confidentially that she'd moved in with a man. He had the largest known private library on gnosticism on the eastern seaboard. It was enormous. But how large does it have to be, I said, to be the largest known etc. And then she got dreamy, which I'd never seen before, only puzzled, and she called him her Big White Bishop. Now get this—not because he was a bishop, although he was, and not because he was white, although he was, very, except for his alarming port-guzzler's schnozz—but because his cock was proportionately as knobful ivory and stiff as the Staunton chess piece of the same name. AND the head of it was correspondingly shapely and exciting and the knob of it all, the mitre, was excitingly sliced, cloven like the Staunton fella's. Boy does that ever get me going, she said there in the cake shop as never before.

We each had a reason for not seeing the other any more: my reason was that she was living with a bishop, and although I wasn't a respecter of persons, I was a respecter of diks, in their place. Her stated reason was that she could no longer discuss gnosticism with me because her research was now private. It couldn't be shared with nongnostics and certainly not paraded in a public cake shop for just anyone to overhear. But you've never told me anything about it, I said. Well, you don't just, she said, I think I've revealed far too much. It was nice seeing you again. I have to dash. That little throb in her voice on the word 'dash'.

TEN YEARS LATER, I was eating Mexican food with my uncle in Los Angeles. He kept putting off the main course and ordering guacamole, because every time you ordered guacamole they wheeled a little cart over to your table and diced, squeezed and squished up the stuff to order, right in front of you; all over you. When are you going to have had enough of this? I said. Look what they did to my shirt. So? said my uncle, big deal. I have a show to do at six-thirty, I said. You going to wear that shirt to work? he said, no wonder your ratings are down. They're up, I said.

My uncle was trying to do too many things at once: to eat guacamole, raise tiresome family issues with me, and to hide both his bulk and his clerical garb behind the table, the napkin and the menu. I don't know why—presumably it's all right to eat Mexican food if you are a clergyman—what the hell do they eat in Mexico? And my uncle was no fatter than anybody else in Los Angeles, and compared to the gigantic Midwestern ministers at the convention he was attending, he was svelte. Svelte.

He wanted me to go back to his hotel with him, so we could telephone my mother to report we'd met up and had a good time, as he always put it, which we certainly hadn't. I had to get to work but I agreed to go to his stupid hotel because otherwise there'd be no end to it. The lobby was full of priests and ministers and frankly I was terrified; my uncle barged his way toward the elevators, shaking hands, slapping this one on the back, swatting another on the butt. What do these people have to be so happy about? I said. My uncle grinned and came out with his 'quiet philosophical' tone of voice. If you have to ask, he said, you'll never know. That's some fucking advertisement, I said. With an attitude like that, aren't you afraid the Baptists are going to steal a march on you? Why should I care what the Baptists do? said my uncle. And watch your language. Well aren't you all in the same business? I said. Are we hell! said my uncle, and as he boomed out the word hell there by the elevators these ministers turned around and here was Nina, of all people, and beside her was her Big White Bishop. Obviously.

Nina? She gave me one of her narrow looks, or perhaps

these days it was a contact lens squint, but it seemed shockingly familiar. Oh, hello, she said, with that little throb. She was dressed very well and was carrying a pair of black leather gloves in her hand. Her hair was perfect and she gave me the wry smile, the one from the cake shop. I had the feeling she couldn't remember my name for the life of her, but then she suddenly used it, in introducing me to the Bishop. We shook hands. My uncle said, Aren't you going to introduce me? Of course, I said, this is Nina. Charmed, said my uncle, you're very pretty. Thanks, she said in a tone of voice that can only be described as weird. And this, I said, is Bishop Staunton. We've met, said my uncle, strangely, and they sneered at each other.

Nina was looking down at her elegant shoes and making a small sniffing noise, which I remembered indicated confusion on her part—she looked back at me and said Well, goodness, what are you doing here? Visiting my uncle, I said, he's some sort of prelate. My uncle smirked at this though he didn't deny it. The elevator doors opened and we all got in. Push twenty-seven, said the bishop to Nina. Hey, that's my floor, said my uncle, we're all on twenty-seven, what do you think about that? The bishop was staring at my uncle, staring at a spot just above my uncle's nose and then at his left temple. Have you exfoliated today? said the bishop uncomfortably. No, said my uncle, have you excommunicated anyone today? None of your business, said the bishop. Why not stop by for a drink with us later? Nina kept looking down at her shoes. Love to, said my uncle. I have to go to work, I said.

The elevator was making a sound of poor maintenance,

like one of the cables had come loose from the pulleys and was whipping around in the shaftway. I'm never comfortable in these things, said my uncle, the hydraulic ones are much safer. He had this RELIGION which was supposed to comfort him, and all he thought about every day was his own death, falling to his death, being flattened, burned, hurled, exploded, jellied or eaten away from the inside. Well, there's no such thing as a thirty-story piston, Unk, I said, so forget it. I wouldn't be so sure about that, said the bishop. He was pretty arch.

We got off at twenty-seven and walked up the hall together. Nina and the bishop paused in front of their room and my uncle waved and trotted on—he'd had quite a few beers and we'd never even got a main course. Perhaps your friend would like to come to the party tonight, said the bishop. Open the door. Nina turned to me, still in her confused state, her key in the lock, there was a lot of eyelash fluttering. Yes, she said, why not—we could catch up. I was surprised at this—I had been used to her brush-offs and her invisibilities, but I accepted, I'd join them after work. You have a spot, said the bishop, touching me on the guacamole. Tonight then, she said, and went through the door, which she had first held open sort of deferentially for the bishop.

My uncle's room was chaos, what a mess was inside his head. I can't find the telephone, he said. Who was that? A friend from New York, I said. The old days, said my uncle. She's a gnosticist, I said. My uncle's face took on a pained expression. Aw, he said, those—oh here it is—let's call your mother.

I felt with conviction that twenty servings of guacamole was not the thing to be driving to work on . . . I just blamed it all on my uncle as that is always so convenient. In the car I thought it was very strange that Nina would come to Los Angeles, even for a convention. The light didn't suit her one bit, I thought. But I never saw anyone from New York any more, so what the hell.

At work, one of the electriciennes was wearing black leather jeans, had on a pair of black gloves, and was hoisting a cyc flood back into place with a pulley attached to the grid, as it had burnt out suddenly and frightened a dog act. The audience was listless because they'd been waiting for three hours in the heat.

The party was in some guy's garage, if you can believe that. Okay so it was a five-car garage, three Mercedes one BMW and a little Alfa Romeo to be exact, which had all been moved out to the courtyard, but a garage nevertheless—the walls with wood risers, tar paper. I know something about garages, I grew up in one: it was a little chilly, but I liked the height of the roof, the sound of rain upon it, the smell of wet redwood.

Nina met me at the side door, handed me a black joint and a glass of white wine which was a little warm for Los Angeles, for a host with the aforementioned automobiles, I thought. Nina, so blessed and so fair, bade me enter . . .

I am not going to dwell on this crap, believe me, except as needs be. If you're not familiar with the Scene, you can easily imagine it. There's an entire race of people out there with dungeons in their garages. They publish very bad magazines about this—they are called *Fake Dungeons Monthly* and *Stupid Looking Dungeon* and *Slobs in Rubber.* The Scene, and these woeful magazines, are littered with the same plywood crosses and stocks, the tar-paper walls—all the junk that's in any California idiot's garage—washing machines, hula hoops—and always the same fifty-year-old guys in the same sweaty zippy rubber hoods, their necks under the scuffed boots of housewife-dominas bored out of their skulls—I mean WOULD YOU GET OUT OF HERE WITH THAT STUFF?

In Los Angeles everything is fake, even the grit. This dungeon garage was decorated with very neat spray-painted graffiti: SPANKERS CORNER. PAIN IS PLEASURE. ABANDON HOPE ALL YE WHO ENTER. KILROY WAS HERE. Whose garage is this? I said to Nina. I've no idea, she said, it doesn't matter. I'm worried that most of these people are from the convention, I said. I don't like ministers.

She was dressed, I thought, exactly as she used to be—all in black, which took from her face what color wasn't absorbed by her dark eyes, her eyelashes and her black hair—her looks in the old cake shop days anticipated the preferred look for girls in the Scene, pale, sculpted, severe. It's an attractive look, I thought, so-o-o, why is it okay that the look for guys is:

1. Fat FACE.
2. BEER belly.

3. Alopecia.
4. Verrucae.
5. Infinitesimal dik that won't work.

For your information, none of this is about sex. At all. What it's about is being a NERD. If these guys didn't have plywood dungeons in their garages, they'd have model trains. Fake trees, little plastic people. The Scene is stupid. It's about childishly *avoiding* sex, and more particularly love. So it's kind of *English* in a way, and maybe that's all you need to know about it. Let me show you around, said Nina.

Can you imagine the feelings of someone from the *eastern seaboard* who finds himself in the middle of all this San-Fernando-rubber-transvestite-stripper-heel-baby-oil-body-makeup-vibrator-blowjob crap? . . . but Nina, that's your situation exactly, isn't it? Ahem . . . I get a little frank when I smoke dope . . . but what is the meaning of this Scene, it has to have a meaning even if it is stupid—that's what Sartre continually bangs on about isn't it? The meaning of things? Even the gnosters were interested in finding out what things meant, except that they were going to keep it all to themselves, whereas Sartre wrote it up for us all to read, if we will . . . so the Gnosts are sort of bad guys, I said, anti-democratic . . . enemies of modernity. Course as anyone in New York will tell you, modernity and democracy are fucking shot . . . man, they're . . . everyone's *jaded*? No one can be bothered to make love properly? . . . can't be ARSED? But why pick on that to the exclusion of poverty, heroin, Republicans? They're all afraid maybe of the big bug and its many little cousins? But really Nina, none of this looks very sanitary . . . look at this guy, he looks like a middle of the night motel manager, toiling away at someone else's rented rubber rectum . . .

I might have said some or all of this

—?—

See that one over there? said Nina, my guide, pointing at a chubby man whose beard looked as if it had no purpose but to catch McDonalds debris. I dated him. He's always got bruises, which he tells his colleagues are the result of accidents in the home, banging his arm in the refrigerator door and so on. So? I said. But that's his thing, said Nina, the refrigerator. He had me dressed up in some pretty uncomfortable things, and I was to slam the fridge door on his arm again and again, have you ever? No, I said, the stupidity washing over me. But still, I thought, take this blonde, her hands and ankles in leather cuffs, leant awkwardly against this hideous home cocktail bar out of Sears-Roebuck from 1962, now painted black— there was something in the way the restraints forced her to stand. Why don't you fuck her until she screams? said Nina. That's what she's here for. Why would I want to do that? I said, she's practically screaming already. With boredom. I suddenly felt that everything, from tickling a testis with a leather mop, to society in general, was something which belonged properly and solely to the school yard.

Have you ever read any real books? I said to the bishop, who'd suddenly appeared at my side. Something elevating?

I'm not sure what you mean by that, he said. Let me show you something. He took Nina by the hand, gave me the blonde's leash to hold, and I followed them, the blonde tiptoeing behind me with difficulty, to the next spectacle, a potbelly strapped down on a black leather piano bench. On the side it said BECHSTEIN, the bench not the belly. Two girls were energetically applying silly-looking plaited cats to his wotzits.

How do you like that? said the bishop.

I studied the situation. I looked at it from several angles. I drew the blonde to me and bade her study the tableau—and only then did I realize that this juddering, putty-colored stomach was attached to the rest of my uncle. Of course, the sight of my uncle always upset me. Well, I said finally, because the bishop really was waiting for an answer, I don't think they're hitting him hard enough.

They say it's good for your sexual machinae to retain your urine until the last possible moment, said my uncle, but I think this is something put about by the larger breweries. Ow!

Listen, you savages, I said, existentialism is an ice cold beer compared to this. This is a huge error.

Existentialism huh, said the bishop. He rolled his eyes at Nina.

This might be erroneous, said my uncle, but it's big. Very big. Ow!

You give people the XXI century and they crave the XIV.

STIFFNESS OF ROPES. FRICTION OF TEETH. FRICTION OF PIVOTS AND COLLARS.

The bishop's day-blouse was purple, with a white dog collar. Now he was wearing a *real* dog collar. So in a way, I thought, everything is in his line: these guys get all the breaks: temporal power, celestial power, orgasms, Nina. How do you plan your whole life out like this, to include everything, from an early age? Are the parents to blame?

Now the Bishop and Nina took me by an arm each and led me to one of the more laughable contraptions in the whole garage, a system of leather cuffs, counterweights and slings. Nina held my balls for me, nicely I thought, while Her Big White Bishop strapped my wrists and ankles into it. He then wound a large leather belt around my waist, such as it is (mine is a sedentary job) and put a bit in my mouth. He gestured to Nina and she went to the garage wall where the ropes were attached to pins. She loosed them and began to haul away, looking remarkably like the electricienne at work, I thought miserably, as I felt myself rising.

When I was a little lad, my mother often told me
Way, haul away, haul away, Joe!
That if I did not kiss the girls, my lips would all grow mouldy
Way, haul away, haul away, Joe!

They'd raised me about seven feet above the concrete floor, its oil stains and stuff that looked like cat litter. *Raising* I've always thought of as an ennobling, gladsome motion. Look at the Amish, their barns and so forth.

The blonde smiled up at me. What we deserve, after all we are put through, is paradise, and paradise alone. To meter it out, to set up a toll booth, is incredible. What about some kindness? Just dump all the cruelty. Forget it. Rise above it.

Take that, said the bishop.

Where is the ice? said a guy in lurex leggings and combat boots, *and he there, how is he fixed thus upside-down?*

I hope you're not going to leave me dangling here, I said.

INCLINED PLANE

Most things castles are not: sinister, haunted, damp, forbidding. I ate the most prosaic sandwich of my life in a 14th century castle. Below the vaulted ceiling I sat in a jumble of folding chairs, disused steam tables shoved up against suits of armor, heraldic banners alternating along the wall with illuminated signs advertising beer. Electrical wires writhed under my feet—the 21st century has to be draped on top of a castle, the way you garland a Christmas tree.

People come to castles like this to get married, to be photographed in an alcoholic haze with their best friends and people they don't like, to have their first married screw in a festooned bed beneath an array of halberds. To begin married life with the *sights and sounds of real medieval battle*.

Castles are an annoyance, a clutter in the landscape, reminding us that we have yet to sort out our society, even our humanity. Castles are places where we now have conferences—large rooms for talks, yes endless *talks* with microphones and power point and prosaic sandwiches. You could say that we have regained the former citadels of aristocratic power. But you would be so wrong. Because what are we always gathering in these castles for? To discuss something that will only pull society further into ruin. But this is where I met her, my one and only true wonderful love, in a castle. Full of name tags.

The place was not without beauty, or a history. There was a deep gorge, many steep paths, even a cave which was available for hermits to rent. The castle was refurbished with an eye to esthetics and comfort: there were real antiques as opposed to fake, the chairs were comfortable, there were a few bath tubs and a telephone.

Here we were supposed to be doing a lot of Thinking About Film, which was impossible due to the lack of a bar and a ban on smoking. There were frequent recesses given, though, during which we stumbled about the castle grounds, our hands clasped behind our backs and our brows as insincerely furrowed as Mussolini's. ('How his face must hurt at night!' one of his *friends* once said.)

Some didn't bother to go out into the ferny, muddy, perplexing policies, but instead returned to their rooms, to send desperate messages in which they begged to be rescued, or even killed, or to plunder bottles, or to jam their heads half way up the chimney and smoke—at dinner these had soot on the tips of their noses.

I was inclined to go out, not because I am any lover of ferns or mud, but because inside there was far too much talk, and outside there was a stream in which I thought a rock might be found. Upon this rock, after clambering or wading to it, I thought I could smoke without being detected, endangering the castle or causing the downfall of civilization.

Far from regretting the worthlessness of the conference, I was furrowing my brow for real, brooding glum on how I had misapprehended the *incline*, how I had floundered mechanically about, for years, at the bottom of the wondrous escarpment of love; how many wedges I had levered into place between me and happiness.

It's no fun to push your cock up the hill of life, I reflected, even if it's on wheels as in rude 18th-century engravings, and mine certainly was not. I thought again about all my dumb mistakes, the wedges I had appeared both to need and to deserve, the problem of supporting my lever, the real male problem of where to fucking *stand*, as Archimedes put it, or would have, if he'd been this pissed off. The pulleys that had snared me, the problem of the simple screw and how to attain it, attain *nothing*, how even *identify* the god damned thing. The spun wheels.

Some say the inclined plane is the real thing, that the wedge is only an application of this truer, simpler machine. Others think the inclined plane is just a wedge you stand on. But the great use of the inclined plane, if you will look at any book on mechanics, is to enable the shifting of a weight which is otherwise impossible. But consider: inclined planes, such as the paths (P) surrounding the castle, also allow us to be drawn down, down, by natural forces such as gravity and ruing—*ruing* can ease you slowly down a ferny slope so you don't splatter yourself into a thousand regretful pieces on the rocks below.

I was nearly, gently then at the foot of the cliff, considering which rock in the stream might not shred my trousers, when there came a cough from above. I looked up and there she was, picking spider webs, spores and frog spawn off her long velvet coat.

I must immediately disabuse you about this coat, since it seems a thing that might cause you chronistical confusion, like the castle. I emphasize that this was in no way a gothic setting. We were assuredly modern confused people who had been flown and driven here; her coat had no air of Stoker or Brontë or Dante—it was a perfectly unhaunted contemporary garment, from a house regularly advertised in *Vogue*.

I stared up at her and she waved and then slowly drew down to my level. I showed her my cigar. I thought that rock out there, I said.

You can take these things too far, she said.

And she was right, I thought. You can take these things too far. This is the first person in years who has said anything so right. There seemed nothing to add. As our 'break' was over, we trudged in silent mutual observation up the incline to the castle.

I thought about her all through the afternoon session: a darkened room, a sandwich, a power point Bozo. She was attending something else, yet another way of Thinking

About Film, something with cinematographers that I now can't recall. But it might not matter what you're doing when you meet your true love. Although if you can remember, it makes a good story for meaningless people like grandchildren.

I said there was no bar, but every day at six o'clock we were supposed to Forgather in the Library for Sherry, doled out to us in plastic thimbles straight from a psychiatric hospital. Sherry—have you ever tasted this stuff? The châtelaine was pleased with herself for doing this: we were meant to feel this was a complimentary bending of the rules, a compromise between Thinking and Life. Whereas, sherry bends nothing. After several days of this, most stopped Forgathering in the Library for Sherry, and those who did came late, having drunk as much as they possibly could in their rooms. I liked the library, now that it wasn't crowded with people Thinking About Film. I got a pleasant feeling there, with firelight on the books, a large window that gave onto the gorge, the châtelaine tickling her spaniel with her toes.

There was an old copy of *Country Life* with an article on the castle kicking around the library. The châtelaine constantly quoted from this article, couldn't she see she said the same thing every day? *The gorge fulfils every expectation of the sublime. The gorge fulfils every expectation of the sublime. The gorge fulfils every expectation of the sublime.* I'll give you gorge! But today the châtelaine and her dog were absent, and they had left MY WOMAN in charge of dribbling out the sherry with the castle micrometer. We began to talk.

I can only describe this way how these things happen: she had just said something amusing and true in regard to our Thinking About Film: *everything was better in black and white*. And she turned away from me. That was it, so simple, the combination of what she said and the unaffected, confident turn of her body before the fire. Perhaps also the quiet of the pretty room? In that moment everything was laid before me—I felt myself being drawn down. Everything had changed. Yet we went on chatting and joking.

At dinner we were seated far apart. This irked me. Even though I now had feelings of hope, security, even pride, that everything in the future was going to be fine, finer than I had ever dared imagine, I resented lending her to others. They were lunkheads. She and I were being *just civilized enough* for them. We were saving our native wits for each other alone.

She *turned away*, I thought.

After dinner everyone drifted off to their rooms, and she and I climbed the stair together, not saying much. I was surprised to find she had the room next to mine. Castles are confusing. But it wasn't only the castle. An ordinary good night confirmed my unshakeable confidence in happiness; for the first time in my life I was going to be happy.

I lay awake, my every atom pining for her to knock softly and come to me, slob that I am. A fear of being, not seen to be, but *of being* a person who tries to fuck at conferences, a *conference fucker*, kept me in my bed. I hoped it was the same for her, but not only that, maybe a shared belief in our inevitable future, a wish not to accelerate or ornament needlessly what was going to happen to us.

The dik pounded.

This woman, I thought, fulfils every expectation of the sublime. What I had yet to realize was that we were both suffering, had always suffered, from the most awful *crippling shyness*. I had an ability to put this out of my mind when it was necessary—one has to function in the world, after all, one has to buy cigars and order beer and tell actors what to do and phona da momma—so you could say I'd got used to being a *fake adult* just in order to stay alive. Here we were, we had met, we had instantly *known*, but now in the dark we were both screaming inside, screaming and ruing, crying out for our lack of boldness, of *savoir-faire*. Lamenting our pasts, o *gods* lamenting them. The mistakes the experiments the louses the vodka tonics the fevered leverings. The redheads. At least that's what *I* was doing, how the hell did I know what she was doing, sleeping, probably. I felt we were already betrothed. By rights we should have met in primary school and been together ever since.

But THEN, I began to flee her. I immediately made commitments which would take me far away. As soon as I got home, I telephoned a woman I barely knew and told her I was moving to her city and that I'd always wanted to have a serious relationship with her. I actually did this.

So against destiny I left the green hilly country she and I thought of as ours, which I now hotly dismissed as old-world and full of bumpkins, and jetted off, snacking panicky on peanuts and whisky, to that place that is very flat and very hot, the home town of course of Not Thinking About Film. And I found it easier, for a time, to push my cock around there, where wheels are the only machine in use—*Hey great wheels man*, they were always saying that. Nobody in this place was inclined to do anything but use his wheels. THESE were the bumpkins!

What I was going to tell you was that I was not running away from my beautiful, inevitable love, never in a million years would I have wanted to do that, in truth it was impossible—what was I, an idiot?—I was running away from the idea that I could have her, the very idea that such a creature existed for me. That I couldn't face and I AM an idiot.

After a few months it dawned on me that the lack of high ground there meant there would never be any impetus, any momentum, any will.

When I was four or five my father would take me to a wonderful park, full of pine and eucalyptus, perched on a hill overlooking our town. This was a churchy town, and a huge grassy amphitheater had been constructed in the park—on Sundays services were held there. Of what nature I never knew, as my father kept me from such things, strictly forbidding me contact with such beliefs, terrifying the pants off me about the whole enterprise, but on Saturdays we could make our way to this steep deep green lawn. He would smoke his pipe and read a newspaper, and I would roll down the grass all the way to the bottom, then run back up the hill dizzy and giggling, the taste of the lawn in my mouth, and launch myself downwards again, like a little rolled-up rug. The incline was very sharp and my father now thinks all this spinning and tumbling down *explains* something about me, something *questionable*, but when I was young I carried the joy of this speed and momentum with me all through the week. I think it the source of the momentum in my life: my smiling father, that dishy hill.

In the flat hot place—Hollywood, if we must give it a name—I came to a dead halt. No one had any inclination to do anything, certainly not examine themselves and how they did nothing, year in and year out. *Art?* Ha. I had no one to tell me what was wrong, that I was hiding my inevitable love from my inevitable love. I had a job many would envy in my 'chosen field'. Bah. If this business is a field, then it's the one with the record number of cow pats.

One day in the middle of a preposterously expensive picture, all sword fights being flown on wires and giant digitized pectoral muscles, set in a castle, a *castle*, there in the dim off the set was an actress in an ornate gown. She was resting on a slant board, which allows you to relax without sitting and crushing a costume like this. She was Italian. Name a hilly place, I said. Napoli, she said.

I called lunch and went over to the Thalberg building. Where is Napoli? I asked the producer. Italy, he said. Near Naples. I quit, I said. You're fired, he said.

I drove home in my wheels, man, and I wrote a letter to my true love, *Everything here has fallen flat. I am inclined to look you up. Let us meet in Napoli.* She wrote back, *Yes.*

I packed my bag and sold my house and took the cat to someone who gave a damn and stopped on my way to the airport to explain to the poor woman I'd been seeing and she set her dog on me, threw the stuff I'd given her out onto the lawn and said that as soon as her daughter got home with her *gun* there'd be nothing left of me and my inclinations, my plots and deceptions. I beat it back to the car in a hailstorm of abuse, bottles of perfume, underwear and hurtful spiky boots.

I was a day in Naples before we met—she'd caught a cold on British Airways, where else, and rang, sniffling, to postpone our meeting, our *love*, for a day. But you cannot postpone the inevitable, I said. *I* said that, who had gone away! She agreed to meet me in the morning at a caffè bar up on the Corso Vittorio Emanuele. From here I took my first real look at the Mediterranean. It's good. But I was really looking up and down the Corso, this way and that—it was past the appointed time. I have waited too long, I thought, she's met someone in the street! Then something soft touched my shoulder; it was the breeze; it was she.

HAIKU: NAPOLI

the girls are all !WHOOSH!
followed by guys with their eyes
the guys are all !DOINGGG!

The whole city of Naples is an astonishing *engine* that turns food, sunlight and noise into love. Up on the plane of the Corso, which curves in and out of the breasts of the hills, there was a tiny filling station, busy with an assortment of gossiping boys and their scooters, smoking, tinkering with their machines, without which one doubts they might live. The hell with America—what would *Italy* do without gasoline?

There's a photograph of the young Sophia Loren adoringly framed or just pasted up in every Neapolitan place of business, her glowing chest looming over a plate of bucatini. Sure, the girls are whoosh!, are pffft!, are vavoomba. As I walked with my true love along the Corso, the *ragazzi* of the filling station sensed her before she was in view, like cats, or birds. Suddenly tense and erect, their sunglasses and haircuts in perfect alignment, they went utterly silent and followed my true love with geared heads, without moving anything else as we passed. Rapt: the cosmic, karmic rays shooting out of them, a Magellanic cloud of beauty surrounding her. We arrived at the funicular ecstatic. We were parts of the engine now.

We sized each other up. I think she liked the look of me, though I was standing in front of one of the largest, most beautiful pasticceria in the world: she kept looking over my shoulder. I didn't care that she had a cold. I no longer cared about the last forty years of my life. I turned to her and solemnly asked her to give me her cold. Cold? she said. I'm planning to give you double pneumonia.

The funicular arrived. Having ascended much of Naples, it seemed we were now to go the most down we could go.

One night during the Second World War, when all in Naples were starving, a band of citizens stormed the aquarium, the oldest in Europe. They netted up every exhibit in the place and had a grand barbecue on the riviera, by the light of torches. For one night, Naples feasted, on *aragosta* and *calamari* and *polpetelli* and a huge horrible antiquarian grouper. And what aquarium other than this would conveniently have had a tank of *sarde*? This made quite an impression on Luigi. He was four. His mother opened a restaurant in 1947 and he still cooks the same way she did that night—on the charcoal, in a hurry, looking over his shoulder.

My true love took my hand and led me down the steps to his place. Are steps never considered a machine? They are a serrated inclined plane. Children may roll down hills, but adults don't roll. We were becoming adults.

In the ristorante it was dark and we couldn't make each other out, but there was no need of further evaluation, though of course I would have enjoyed to continue to look at her after these stupid months. Luigi presented us, unasked, with a plate of *gamberi alla griglia*.

She talked about the green hilly country. She was slightly fed up with it. Those people *live* like shrimp, she said. They are curled and pink, grasping and tickling with little feelers, getting the BBC through their antennae, sucking slender nourishment from their surroundings. I'm tired of them.

Excellent.

We ate Luigi's spaghetti vongole and washed it down with shimmering white wine from Ischia. We strolled along the riviera and then went back up the steep streets and stairs of the city, toward the bed.

We sank down, naturally down on it. One is drawn, drawn down, by love. Maximum down.

Making love in the wardrobe mirror, canted forward so she could grasp the edge of it; we had both firmly grasped the edge of something. The afternoon light of the Mediterranean through the white curtains, her *scarpe* of red.

The evening was approaching with its time of mini bar and traffic. We stepped onto the balcony, into the real beginning of our *conversazione*. And here we discovered the second most agreeable pastime in the world: watching the auto traffic of Naples. The traffic was tricolore, with some black and blue thrown in. There was much drama, comedy, bravura! The beeping wedges and phalanxes of the bold chancers! This diverting, skittish molecular motion put me in mind of my past, as we stood on the balcony with our drinks and our undeniable love, and it was far below me.

My true love said, I think there is a system to this, though it is a system without laws. I thought about it yesterday. It's based on a series of macro- and micro-historical entitlements. See that guy in the red Fiat? He's allowed to pull out now because he has been waiting for more than twenty seconds, he is related by marriage to a formerly well-to-do family, and his Fiat is red. And the others are able to divine all that by the merest glimpse of his face, she said, and look, there he goes! It works. Like everything in Naples.

Come on, she said. When we went inside again there was something crazy to it, looking into each other's eyes in the mirror, something we'd learned from the *macchini*, random, darting and edgy. It worked. Man, did it work. The piston, I said to her, has always seemed a *fairly* simple machine.

From that star, our bright room in Napoli, we have gone no longer shyly down the streets of our *conversazione*. There has been trudging, up, but always a drawing down. We have gone down through hangers of English beech, above which perched our bedroom; down the steep streets of Edinburgh, down ancient steps in Sperlonga and Stromness. Down Broadway. Everything with my true love has been steep, steep our love, steep our inclination.

On my desk sits a little carving she made me, the two of us twined in sleep. She made this, my inevitable love, with her own hands—and not a gadget or a gizmo or a machine in sight.

Ⓑ *editions*

Founded in 2007, CB editions publishes chiefly short
fiction (including work by Gabriel Josipovici, David
Markson and Dai Vaughan) and poetry (Fergus
Allen, Andrew Elliott, Beverley Bie Brahic, Nancy
Gaffield, J. O. Morgan, D. Nurkse). Writers published
in translation include Apollinaire, Andrzej Bursa,
Joaquín Giannuzzi, Gert Hofmann and Francis Ponge.

Books can be ordered from www.cbeditions.com.